Tales from the Wood

A Modern Fairytale

R.A. Johnson

CROW Books

Cover art and interior illustrations by Anthony Moravian.

Illuminated letters courtesy of Vandy Pacetti-Donelson.

An audio version of this book, narrated by Naomi Mayo, is also available.

Second Edition
July 2023

eBook ISBN 978-1-959480-00-6
Audiobook ISBN 978-1-959480-01-3
Amazon paperback ISBN 978-1-959480-02-0
Amazon hardcover ISBN 978-1-959480-03-7
General distribution paperback ISBN 978-1-959480-05-1
General distribution hardcover ISBN 978-1-959480-06-8

For Ona.

Even though you weren't a fan of my writing, and wouldn't listen to my favorite band, I still love you dearly.

PREFACE

Hi. R.A. Johnson here. Let me give you a little background about this book and what inspired it.

I first saw the band Jethro Tull at Madison Square Garden when I was a sophomore (second year) in college in 1978. I think I'm up to ten shows of either Tull or Ian Anderson solo since then. Why am I telling you this? Because my love of Tull's music, and especially Mr. Anderson's lyrics, inspired the little book you're holding now.

I hadn't heard of Jethro Tull, or any progressive rock band for that matter, when my brother Ed brought home a copy of the album "Songs from the Wood" shortly after its release in 1977. Like the woman in the story that follows, I felt transported to a different time and place as I listened to its magical lyrics, lilting melodies, and strange key signatures. It still has that effect on me, and it has become a go-to soundtrack for my writing sessions, placing it close to the top of my all-time favorites list.

The nine songs on the original album, augmented by another on the 2003 Remastered edition, have always stuck in my mind as a set of tales one might hear around the campfire on a pilgrimage to, say, Canterbury. Recently, I needed a short story for a competition, and I decided I would, after over four decades of rumination, weave the songs into a single narrative. Alas, as I should have known would happen, the through-line of Cindy's adventures grew beyond a short story into the novella before you now, but that gave me the opportunity to publish this modern fairytale, with its beautiful illustrations by Anthony Moravian, as a standalone volume.

Each chapter is a tale which takes its core story from a song on the album, though slightly out of order in some cases. I've done my best to build a hopefully compelling story around them populated by quirky companions, duplicitous villains, magical creatures, and one young woman trying to make sense of it all.

I strongly encourage you, Faithful Reader, to give the album a listen. The 2003 Remastered version includes a song to go along with each of these chapters. I strongly recommend that you listen to that version of the album as companion background tracks. Make a playlist that includes the songs that match the chapters in this order:

1:	*Song from the Wood*	"Songs from the Wood" [1]
2:	*Jack Green*	"Jack-in-the-Green" [2]
3:	*The Wondrous Cup*	"Cup of Wonder" [3]
4:	*Lady of the Hunt*	"Hunting Girl" [4]
5:	*May Day*	"Beltane" [10]
6:	*Spring's Rare Delights*	"Velvet Green" [6, 11]
7:	*Bell's of Summer*	"Ring Out, Solstice Bells" [5]
8:	*Whistler's Tune*	"The Whistler" [7]
9:	*Steps of a Lifetime*	"Pibroch (Cap in Hand) [8]
10:	*Midnight Embers*	"Fire at Midnight" [9]

You can listen to each track on repeat while reading its companion. After all, that's how I wrote them. Of course, if you're listening to this as an audiobook, take a break and listen to the album now, so you don't interrupt Naomi Mayo's wonderful narration.

Faithfully,

R.A. (Rob) Johnson
Pennsylvania, U.S.A.
July 2023

Chapter 1

Song from the Wood

The big old house's library was packed floor to ceiling, but not with books, though many of the thousands of its denizens told stories of love and loss, joy and heartache. Some simply made you tap your foot and smile. Still others could bring tears to the eyes of even the most stoic, without a single word.

The ancient, dark wooden shelves seemed to groan under the weight of the burdens they had borne for so many decades.

"There sure are a lot of them," Cindy said. She sat in a straight-back chair before a massive mahogany desk. It was a chair she sat in many times before as she grew up from a little girl to a twenty-something woman. It had been a good ten years since her last visit, though.

A stranger sat in the desk chair this time. He nodded. His three-piece suit was out of place in this realm of the dim and distant, dusty past.

He should've worn tweed, Cindy thought, remembering the many times she had squirmed in this very chair.

The lawyer cleared his throat. "Your grandfather was very proud of his collection. Some of these recordings are extremely rare."

Cindy barely heard the words. The memories those towering shelves evoked were too distracting.

Pops always wore that ratty old tweed sport coat with the patches at the elbow, she thought.

"He was very proud of you as well. He often talked about you and how you would tell each other stories when you visited."

Cindy smiled, reminiscing despite herself. "We did. Fantastic stories." Memories of Pops telling her tales so full of detail that, as a child, she lost herself in the magical world they shared.

But then she snapped back to the present and waved her hand. "As you can see, he took things to the extreme."

She pointed at various objects around the room. A carving of the Green Man from folklore glowered from high up in each corner of the room. A gold amulet, he claimed he pulled from a peat bog, rested under a glass dome on one shelf. Paintings of fairies and nymphs, spirits and demons, hung about the room.

Looking more closely, she muttered, "They could use a good cleaning."

"Indeed, your grandfather had trouble keeping assistants. They only seemed to last a few months or so…until the last one. Ian, I think his name was. He took good care of your grandfather until—until he just disappeared one day."

The lawyer shrugged, then leaned forward across the desk. "He missed you. A great deal, I suspect, though he would never admit it. Even so, you could tell from the way he spoke of your visits. He worried, too. He worried that you might have lost your way."

Shattered dreams—a cheating husband—will do that to you. I should have…I don't know. Something.

Cindy felt things she had suppressed for a long time. Guilt. Regret. Shame. And a new feeling of loneliness and loss.

She thought, *He's gone and I'll never be able to see him again, to tell him I'm sorry. The visit that I've put off for so long will never happen now. No more fantasies shared in front of the fireplace.*

The lawyer cleared his throat to bring her back to reality, then continued, "The appraisers have valued the entire musical library at between two and three million, but you could probably get three or four times that if you split it up."

That got her attention.

"Wait. Two or three million? Dollars?"

"At a minimum. I can recommend—"

Her mind raced. *That would pay off my loans, and credit cards, and… Wait. This is Pops we're talkin' about.*

"And he left them all to me?"

"He did…under one condition."

Her expression revealed her thoughts. *I knew there was a catch. With Pops, there was always a catch. And I bet I know what it is.*

"Of course, there's a 'condition.' What is it?"

The lawyer stood and took two steps to the wall behind the desk. He reached up and pulled down an LP that held pride of place among the thousands of albums, forty-fives, and seventy-eights.

I knew it.

"He tried to get me to listen to that thing a dozen times," she muttered, but kept the rest of her thoughts to herself.

That's why I stopped coming. He seemed obsessed with it. It was creepy.

The album sleeve was scuffed and worn, but its cover picture still showed what looked like a bad museum tableau of a medieval campfire scene. The lawyer held it almost reverently. Cindy felt her stomach clench when she imagined what her grandfather's condition might be.

"Your grandfather specified in his will that nothing transfers to you until you listen to this album in its entirety."

Her surprise was obvious when she said, "That's it? I don't have to dance around a Maypole or draw ancient runes and chant in some forgotten language?"

The lawyer chuckled. "Nope. Just listen to this record."

Relief flowed through her, though tinged with suspicion. *Still...*

"Ah, forty minutes of my time is certainly worth a couple mil."

Cindy opened a music app on her phone and pulled earbuds from her purse.

"No," the lawyer said, "you don't understand. You need to listen to *this* recording."

He carried the record, cradled in his hands like a precious religious icon, to the highest-end audio system Cindy had ever seen. Placing the vinyl on the turntable, he carefully washed and dried the first side, then indicated an overstuffed armchair. Cindy abandoned the wooden guest chair and gratefully settled into the much more comfortable seat. Then he handed her a set of studio quality headphones.

"You must listen with these. I will flip to the other side when necessary."

She shrugged. "Seems like overkill, but sure."

She settled the headphones over her ears and gave the lawyer a jaunty thumbs up. Silence reigned for a moment, followed by a second or two of scratchy noise. When the words and music burst forth, they filled her being. The melody caught her mind and sent it spinning. Images formed that belied her presence in the stuffy library. She saw verdant valleys and primeval forests. She heard birdsong and the skittering of woodland creatures darting through the high grass. Cool breezes kissed her cheeks and wafted scents of wood smoke and honeysuckle to her nose.

The singers' voices entranced her while their contrapuntal harmonies painted a picture of a hard life well lived in a mythical time and place. The invitation was clear: "Come join us for an adventure, a celebration, laughter, love, and maybe even a little danger."

She might have resisted the voices, the guitars, drums, and tinkling bells, but the flute…ah the flute dove straight into her subconscious with its haunting notes and trills. Its calling was irresistible. By the end of the first verse, Cindy's perception of the dark library faded, and a new reality took its place. When the second verse finished, the world of the here-and-now was gone and she found herself transported to a darkening forest, where a chilling wind blew down from snow-capped mountains.

Her jeans and sweater were likewise transformed into heavy woolen breeches tucked into calf-high boots, a scratchy shirt two sizes too big, and a leather jerkin laced with a rough-cut thong. As if in a dream, Cindy accepted these changes as matters of fact.

The music was gone, but the world it created had become her reality.

#####

Where am I, and how the heck did I get here? A gust of wind blew a chill through Cindy. *And why aren't I freaking out right now?*

The flute's earworm echoed in her mind, keeping her panic at bay. It already seemed familiar—as if she had been listening to it for years and knew every note by heart.

Maybe I have been. Pops always had music playing when I visited.

Cindy looked around, examining every tree, every branch, every leaf. She stood at the edge of a track with a single pair of wheel ruts, barely wide enough for a wagon, that wound its way through the woods. Birds twittered high in the trees and squirrels darted along the branches that formed an arching tunnel overhead.

If this is a dream or a hallucination, the details are incredibly real. She bit down on her tongue and was rewarded with a sharp pain. *Not a dream, then. Can't feel pain in a dream. A hallucination, maybe?*

She waved her hand furiously in front of her face. It left no trails of color behind.

Not an acid trip, either. In fact, her senses felt sharper than they ever had. She picked out four different birdsongs. The bitterness of pine mingled in her nose with the sweetness of beech, underlaid by the rich earthy, yet somehow comforting smell of the loam on the forest floor.

Pleasant as the setting was, Cindy was not the type to live her life in a dream.

OK, this is fun, but it's time to wake up from this…whatever this is.

Being lucid during a dream was nothing new to Cindy. She was often aware of her dreams while still in them. Over the years, she had learned different mental exercises for directing the course of the more fantastical ones, while also being able to wake herself up from her not-infrequent nightmares.

She bit down harder on her tongue. Nothing happened except another sharp pain. She stretched her face, opening her eyes as wide as possible—nothing. She even slapped herself hard enough for the sound to echo down the forest trail. Confused, she was about to let out her loudest shout when she noticed fresh sounds interrupting the flute, still playing in her head.

The tinkling of the bells was first to catch her notice, but once she paid attention, the clop-clop of a horse's hooves became clear, as did the rattle of wooden wheels on the rutted track. Doubt and fear flooded Cindy's thoughts. Whether a dream, hallucination, or something else entirely, she seemed unable to escape it, and that scared her.

Reacting without thinking, she dove off the hard-packed track into the undergrowth. Hiding behind a thorn bush, Cindy watched as a wagon pulled by a single horse came around a bend in the road. The horse was huge. Its body, with muscles flexing and straining under its heavy load, was a tawny brown. A long mane of golden yellow blew in the breeze. Long, feathery hair grew from his lower legs and flopped hypnotically as he plodded along.

Riding atop the wagon was the driver, whose arms and legs looked like he could pull the wagon himself. A long, scraggly beard spilled out of the hood that covered his head, so she could see only his eyes and his wide smile. Despite his imposing frame, Cindy liked the look of him.

Next to the driver sat the object of every one of Cindy's fantasies.

Now I know *I'm dreaming.*

The rider sat tall, equal in height if not in girth, to the mountain of a man driving the wagon. His hood was thrown back, revealing his long, flowing locks that shimmered in the late afternoon sun. A ray of sunlight passing through the overhanging branches, illuminated his movie star features, and Cindy's heart melted.

He's...gorgeous.

There was no other word for it. Simply gorgeous.

As the wagon approached, she could see that fading paint decorated it with crude pictures of musical instruments. A lute-type thing—almost a guitar—danced in a circle with a brass horn, a fiddle, a flute, and assorted drums. Strings of tiny bells hung from the corners of the wagon, tinkling as it rocked back and forth.

When the wagon drew abreast of Cindy's hiding place, the rider called out, "Hey, Whistler, play a tune that will make this old nag pick up the pace. It's gettin' on ta dark."

As if insulted by the name calling, the horse stamped a hoof, snorted, and whinnied in protest.

Calls of "Aye," and "Hear, hear!" came from two other members of the troupe, who walked along behind the wagon. Cindy heard a reluctant sigh come from somewhere. Then it started. The song that had wormed its way into Cindy's head, the sound of the very flute that echoed in the back of her mind, sang out through the gathering dusk.

The horse picked up his pace, and the walkers added a bounce, almost a dance, to their step amongst smiles and nods. Cindy peered after the wagon as it passed, searching for the source of the haunting melody without success until the troupe had almost reached the next bend in the beaten track.

Silhouetted by the sinking sun, a figure sat up atop the wagon. The feather in his cap cut the sun in half, and he held a flute to his lips as his fingers danced along its length. In the last light of the setting sun, as the wagon turned out of sight, Cindy glimpsed the player's face staring straight at her hiding place. A smile curled the corner of his lip as their eyes locked. Then the wagon was gone, though his song continued.

Cindy sat frozen in her hiding spot until all sounds of the wagon, the horse, and the Whistler had faded to be replaced by the natural sounds of the forest creatures, the rubbing of swaying tree branches, and the rustling of their leaves.

What do I do now? Should I have flagged them down? Should I run to catch up with them? I'm a lone woman—dressed like a man—in this strange place. A chilly breeze ruffled her hair. *And it's getting cold—and dark.*

The chilly breeze broke her paralysis, and she rose from her hiding place. The lessons Pops taught her on their many camping trips came back unbidden.

Shelter first, water next, then food.

She could follow the track. The troupe of musicians would camp somewhere along the way, probably not too far ahead. Something told her, though, that the more she interacted with this world that she found herself in— wherever and whenever it was—the more real it would become. And the harder it would be to get home.

Instead of following the wagon, she turned into the forest.

The fading light showed her a game trail that led her deeper into the woods until she found a place to spend the night. It was a stand of hemlocks, their broad, flat branches hanging down to the mossy forest floor. A small stream tinkled over rocks close by. With no better options, Cindy lifted a heavy branch and crawled under.

Sure enough, as she expected, the long, overlapping branches formed a tent out of the wind. The ground was dry, and if not warm, at least the thick moss softened it a bit. Cindy curled up between the knees of two roots and took stock.

Shelter—check. Water—close by. I'll find it in the morning. Food? I'll worry about that tomorrow. Tomorrow, I need to figure out what the heck is going on.

The sweet smell of the hemlocks, the susurration of the breeze through their branches, and her surprisingly comfortable billet combined to weigh heavily on her eyelids. Despite the fear and confusion of the past hour, or perhaps because of it, Cindy fell into a deep sleep.

Chapter 2

Jack Green

"Hey, now. What is this?"

Cindy startled awake at the sound of the squeaky voice. She lay curled up where she fell asleep, but now the lowest branches of the hemlock that formed her bedstead were bent low, covering her like a warm, soft blanket.

Getting her bearings took a moment, and when she did, she pushed further back against the warm, inviting tree. Illuminated by the early morning sun streaking through the forest, the head of some creature Cindy had never seen before poked into her hiding place.

As green as the rest of the forest, the face was that of an old man, but leaves of every kind, rowan, oak, holly, and more, grew from his tall forehead and fell in cascades to his shoulders. One side of his not-hair was tucked behind a pointed ear.

"I say, who are ye and why are ye here?" He sounded grumpy, but not overtly hostile.

Still panicked and astounded by the appearance of something straight out of her dreams, Cindy couldn't find

15

her voice. Instead, the hemlock's branches whispered in response.

The creature cocked his head, listening to their plea, then nodded. "A lost young lass, then? You're dressed oddly for such."

Cindy found she could nod, at least.

"Quiet thing, ain't ya?"

Taking strength from the comfort of the hemlock's protective branches, Cindy found her voice. "Not normally. But…" She choked on a sob as the fantastical nature of the situation collided head-on with her rational mind.

"There, there," the green creature said, his voice a lot less threatening.

Cindy's protective hemlock opened her branches to reveal the rest of the green man standing in the sun. About three feet tall, he wore a hooded gown of moss woven throughout with tendrils of vine from which sprouted leaves of every sort and berries of every color. His posture was that of someone more ancient than any of the trees he lived to protect. His likeness, and its promise of rebirth, were carved into wood and stone since the days before there was a language in which to write his story. He leaned heavily on a gnarled staff of hazel; his back bent nearly double.

"Where be my manners? I been known by many names, but you can call me Jack Green, or just Jack, if ya prefer."

He gave a sweeping bow, bending the rest of the way until his forehead nearly touched the ground.

Calmed by his manner, Cindy found her voice. "Hello, Jack. I'm Cindy." She stood, and Auntie Hemlock pulled back her blanket of branches. "Pleased to meet you." She hesitated, then continued, "Pops—my grandfather—told me you were just an old mythical symbol."

Jack chuckled, which set the leaves on his head rustling. "Symbol, or myth, or not, here I be. Which raises the question, what be you doin' here?"

She took a deep breath, but no words came, as she had no answer. Jack cocked his head, listening again.

"Auntie Hemlock says you talk in your sleep. A dangerous habit in these parts, I'd say. Secrets are best kept just that—secret." He listened to the swaying branches again. "So, ye have no more idea how you came to be here than I do?"

Cindy shook her head. "No. I was listening to music, then…poof. Here I was, dressed like this."

Jack frowned and Auntie Hemlock's branches sagged lower.

"So, it's come to that, eh?" He shook his head, sending his leaves rustling again, but this time there was a note of sadness in their tone.

"What do you mean? *What* has come to that?"

Instead of an answer, Jack looked into Cindy's eyes unblinkingly. After a moment, he nodded to the tree's murmuring.

"You didna' come here of your own will, then?" Cindy shook her head. "And you just want to go back?" She nodded. His eyes bored into hers. "To what?"

Startled, Cindy found she couldn't answer.

After a moment, Jack asked again, "To what? A pleasant home in the country?" Cindy thought of the tiny apartment she could barely afford and shook her head. "A loving husband, then?" Cindy said nothing. "A lover, perhaps?"

More like the hassles and questions of a broken marriage, she thought.

"Dear friends and family?"

Friends, yes, but dear ones?

Out loud, she said, "Pops was my only family."

Feeling more alone than she had in her whole life, losing her dreams for her future, and worse, losing her grandfather, sent silent tears flowing down her cheeks. Auntie Hemlock embraced her again and gathered her close to her trunk.

Jack frowned, but was stern. "What do ye have to go back to, then? Why not stay here?"

Cindy wiped the tears from her cheeks. "But where is here? *What* is here?"

Jack smiled ruefully. "Look 'round ya'. You know this *here*. You've seen it in your mind's eye your whole life long."

It was true. Her lack of panic, her understanding to seek Auntie Hemlock's embrace, even her lack of shock at this strange Jack Green creature she was having a conversation with told her how familiar the setting was.

"So, this is just a fantasy? It isn't real?"

"Oh, ho! That's the toughest question of all. Seems to me it's as real as the life you thought you'd have back *there*. More real now, I s'pose."

"How—what happened to me? How is this possible?" Cindy felt panic rising in her throat.

"How? Why, it be magic, me dear."

Magic. Magic?

"But I was just listening to old music." She thought for a moment. "A song describing this place, this world."

"There is that, yes." He nodded and tapped his staff on the ground. "Then this is not just *your* dream world. It is someone else's but close enough to yours, so here ye be."

Cindy shuddered. "You mean I got sucked into someone else's fantasy?"

Jack listened to Auntie Hemlock again. "Aye, could be." Then he said to Cindy, "Maybe ye was summoned here. Like your dreams were singin' in harmony with someone else's. And now, here ye be."

Cindy felt violated. "So, someone lured me here? Some predatory creep?"

"Lured or brought by luck? That I can'a say."

She scoffed. "Luck? How is this lucky? But more to the point, how do I get back home?"

Jack's tone carried the weight of his next question. "*Back* or *home*? Which is it you want more?"

Cindy opened her mouth to respond with a sharp retort, but then the import of his question crashed like a wave onto the shore. It took her several slow, deep breaths before she responded.

"Home. I want to find a home. Whether it's back *there*, or somewhere else, I want a *home*. I want to go home."

Jack nodded and smiled. Auntie Hemlock sighed knowingly.

"I canna' tell ya' what your path home is, or where it will take ya' other than this," he said. "Your path lies through your heart."

The rightness of his words resonated through her whole being, but her rational self couldn't help asking. "Which way do I go?"

Jack's laugh was echoed by the rubbing of Auntie Hemlock's branches. "Following that tune in your head might be a good way to start."

I don't know why I'm dressed like this, but I'm glad I have pants on and not some long, flowing skirt, she thought as she jogged along the forest track.

She stopped occasionally to drink when a stream was close by, and to listen for the sound of the troupe's wagon. Her boots fit her feet perfectly, and the thick leather soles protected them from any jagged stones along the path. A following breeze kept her cool and even seemed to grow in strength to lend a helping hand whenever she had a hill to climb.

Those cardio classes must be working. I've been jogging along for hours and haven't even gotten winded.

She skidded to a halt.

Wait a minute. I'm not tired—I'm not even sweating. I'm not hungry even though I haven't eaten for a day. And my feet don't hurt.

The breeze at her back strengthened.

And I met a magical creature who gave me advice—cryptic advice, true—but Jack did tell me which way to go, at least. Whoever or whatever brought me to this place, this world, seems to have a plan.

The breeze became a wind that blew in gusts strong enough to make Cindy wobble on her feet.

"Wait a minute," she yelled. "Let me think this through."

The wind stopped as quickly as it had started.

"Thank you." A light breeze ruffled her hair, bringing the hint of a smile to her face.

What are my options?

She looked left and right, but all she could see on either side of the rutted path was a dense forest.

Either forward toward a group of scruffy-looking strangers, or back to where I started and hope there's a way out of here in that direction.

She felt the breeze switch around and blow through the strands of hair that had escaped her hat, cooling her face.

"You want me to go back?"

A powerful gust struck her in the middle of her back, while the gentle breeze continued to caress her face.

"How can you blow from both directions at once?"

She heard the now-familiar sound of hemlock branches rubbing out a message: "Sssshhh."

OK, then.

Keeping quiet, she felt the breeze on her face grow in strength a little and the trees at her sides fall silent. Carried to her by the guiding breeze, she heard the tinkling of bells and a flute playing low.

They're close.

"Thank you," she whispered to the wind and started forward again.

Chapter 3

The Wondrous Cup

Interspersing a light jog with a good walking pace, by late afternoon Cindy drew within earshot of the horse's hooves beating a steady pattern against the hard-packed ground. Keeping out of sight, but always within the sound of the troupe, she followed them until the sun had dipped close to the mountains that flanked them on their left.

The steady plodding of the draft horse and rumbling of the wagon's wheels became the sounds of the troupe laughing and calling out as they pitched their tent and scoured the forest for firewood. Cindy took to the forest herself, staying hidden within Auntie Hemlock's embrace until it was near dark. The smell of wood smoke roused her from her hiding place, and she crept within eyesight of them.

They had chosen a perfect spot to set their camp. A meadow stretched from the road down a gentle slope to a brook that tumbled along its way toward its wider brethren. Wildflowers dotted the meadow, peaking their colorful heads above the low grass that still lay dormant after the long winter. The last rays from the sleepy sun poked through a rift in the clouds. Crocuses, daffodils, snowdrops, and creeping mint dotted the field with pink, yellow, white, and blue.

A woman, dressed in a long shift and jerkin like Cindy's walked through the meadow, bending occasionally to pluck a bloom or pinch off a sprig of leaves, lifting the latter to her nose before dropping them in a wicker basket hung over one arm.

They've probably been this way many times…now why would I know that?

Bursts of music—the same flute from earlier—floated on the breeze up from the stream where it bordered the meadow. Cindy felt the pull of the music as if it reached directly into her soul, summoning her to attend its lilting tune. As she rose from where she knelt in hiding, the music stopped abruptly, replaced by splashing sounds followed by hearty laughter.

Cindy quickly dropped back to her knees.

What the heck? Keep your head in the game.

The same pattern of music, splashing, and laughter followed twice more, but she resisted its call and kept to her hiding place.

The giant of a man she saw earlier driving the wagon strode up from the stream, a large bucket sloshing water back and forth in each hand. Beside him walked the man who had lain atop the wagon playing his flute, which was slung by a leather thong across his back, and he carried three good-sized trout strung on a cord.

As the two drew abreast of her, Cindy watched as the flute player dipped his head and glanced in her direction. She froze, holding her breath until they had passed, but the last red ray of sunlight caught his mouth twitch into a tiny smile.

"Ho, ho! Three fine fishes for the fire."

Cindy was so focused on holding still that the bellowing voice nearly made her jump. Walking toward the pair was the man she saw riding on the wagon next to the driver.

Mr. Gorgeous.

The finest sculptor could have carved his face. He had long, light brown hair, with sun-kissed blonde highlights tucked behind his ears, framing a high forehead. His eyebrows, mostly blonde, arched in permanent laughter, as if he had just heard a bawdy joke, and had his own ready in response. A long straight nose stood proudly above his full lips, drawn back in a wide smile which revealed perfect white teeth. All this Cindy took in with a single glance, but his eyes—the brilliant blue of his eyes captivated her, and she felt a flutter in her belly that she hadn't known since college, something she had never felt with Tom, her former husband.

Whoa! Cool your jets. He's probably some creeper.

As the pair returning from the stream approached this Medieval Adonis, the flute player cocked his head and nodded in her direction. The two carrying their burdens continued toward the camp, but the one who embodied the object of Cindy's fantasies looked directly at her and, with an extended hand, motioned for her to come out into the open. She hesitated until a breeze came from nowhere and Auntie Hemlock's branches practically shoved her out into the open field. The smile that broke across his face was like the dawning of a new day for Cindy.

This place ain't so bad after all.

Without thinking, she took his beckoning hand and walked with him into the camp.

"Look what I found," he called as the two approached the warm glow of the campfire. The big wagon driver turned from where he was hanging a bucket of water for the horse. He tipped the floppy, shapeless hat he wore, and the horse bobbed his head twice before returning to slurping water from the bucket.

The woman whom Cindy had seen gathering herbs and flowers stood in the wagon's back door with hands on hips. She had her jet-black hair pulled back in a thick braid, and her brown face formed a scowl.

"You shoulda' caught another fish," she muttered before turning back into the dark wagon.

A fifth member of the troupe, one Cindy had seen walking behind the wagon, stood atop it. He threw a heavy canvas bundle down to the flute player.

"How do, young lady?" he said. "May we know your name?"

"Ah, I'm Cindy," she stammered.

"Cindy, is it? Like Cinderella, I take it. A good story, that one."

Before she could tell him her name was Cynthia, not Cinderella, he spoke again.

"We're not big on actual names here in this troupe. At least one of us," he looked accusingly at the one who still held Cindy's hand, "would rather keep their past in the past."

The driver swapped the water bucket for a pouch of oats, which he fitted over the horse's mouth and looped its thong around its neck.

"Aye, more'n one of us, I 'spect." He tipped his cap again. "You can call me Driver, Missy, 'cause that's what I do. 'Course you could call me Farrier, or Groom, too." He patted the horse's neck. "'Cause I do them jobs, too. This here's Horse," he looked quizzical for a moment. "Never thought to give him any other name."

He turned back, slid a stiff-bristle brush onto his hand, and stroked it along Horse's flank, getting a satisfied rumble in response.

"I'm Bard, your poor storyteller." The man atop the wagon made a deep, sweeping bow before climbing down to the ground. "You've met Chanteur. He can charm a nightingale with his singing." Chanteur gave her hand a squeeze and a steamy look from under his perfectly arched brows. Cindy felt her belly quiver again, then she blushed and turned away.

"The sullen *lady* who keeps us all on the straight and narrow," he pounded on the side of the wagon several times until the black-haired woman reappeared in the doorway, "is none other than Coryphee." He leaned forward with his hand to the side of his mouth and spoke in *sotto voce*, "Don't call her 'Cory,' no matter what. Not if you don't want your throat slit in the night."

Coryphee shook her head, scowled even deeper, and ducked back into the wagon.

"And finally, we have Whistler, the finest *flautist* in all the land."

Whistler rolled his eyes at Bard, nodded curtly to Cindy, and returned to gutting the fish.

"Do ya' play?" Bard asked as he began slicing carrots and potatoes from a sack and dropping them into a pot boiling next to the fire.

"Play?"

"Yah, blow? Strum? Sing? Dance? Tap on a drum?"

Not since clarinet in high school, she thought but just said, "Ah, no."

Bard frowned and Driver looked over Horse's back, a look of surprise on his face. Chanteur lifted her hand and looped it over her head. Cindy obediently did her best dance twirl under their arms.

"I do believe we can find a use for you." His leer broke the spell.

Cindy stumbled backwards and shook her hand free of his. Frightened, she looked around the camp. Driver turned and stepped quickly around Horse. Bard reached for a knife strapped to his calf. Whistler stood but made no move toward her. Seeing no easy route to run from the circle they formed, she confronted Chanteur.

"Whoa, Mr. Creepy. I just want to get home."

Whistler let loose an ear-piercing whistle, and all heads spun in his direction. He met Chanteur's stare with one of his own. They exchanged no words, but when Whistler looked at Driver and Bard in succession, they simply nodded.

Now understanding the situation, she thought, *They were coming to* protect *me.*

Whistler turned back to Chanteur and gave a firm shake of his head. The leer disappeared and the big man stepped back and bowed deeply.

"My apologies, m'Lady. I had no intention of giving offense." Whistler roughly cleared his throat, and

Chanteur continued, "Nor did I mean anything…untoward." He bowed again, this time much more stiffly, then turned on his heel and marched into the encircling darkness.

Bard and Driver returned to their duties, and Whistler laid six filets on a flat griddle suspended above the fire. The sizzle and scent of roasting fish made Cindy's mouth water.

Relieved, Cindy thought, *Now you're hungry? You just avoided being assaulted, and you're hungry? That does smell delicious, though.*

Coryphee emerged from the wagon and tossed a pouch to Whistler, then sewed the herbs she had gathered from the meadow to a cord strung along the back of the wagon. Whistler sprinkled bits of dried leaves onto the sizzling fish. The resulting aroma brought Driver, Bard, and Coryphee to sit cross-legged within the circle of firelight. The other woman caught Cindy's eye and patted the ground next to where she sat.

Forced to choose between running alone into the darkness or sitting by a warm fire, eating a hearty meal, and enjoying the camaraderie and protection of her newfound friends, she plopped onto the soft ground.

The fish and soup were delicious. Cindy sopped up the last with a piece of dark bread broken from a loaf that Coryphee brought from the wagon. With a round of satisfied sighs, the troupe made quick work of cleaning up.

Driver washed off a flat rock among those that ringed the campfire and transferred the one remaining filet to it.

Cindy turned to Whistler. "How did you catch these fish without a rod or a line, or even a hook?"

Whistler raised an eyebrow but remained silent. Bard chuckled and said instead, "He can do magic with that flute," as if that explained anything and everything.

Yeah? Maybe he can whistle me up a cab to take me home.

Eyeing the leftover filet, Cindy said, "Chanteur never came back."

Driver huffed, a sound that could have come from his charge, Horse. Bard leaned back and lit a clay pipe. The aroma of something stronger than tobacco mingled with the wood smoke of the dying fire.

"He's off a'wandrin'," Coryphee replied.

"Not unusual," Bard said.

Driver huffed again, then stood and crossed to where Horse was tethered.

"G'night, my friend," he said as he scratched Horse's withers. The big beast responded by nuzzling his long nose against Driver's neck.

Whistler, who was mostly silent throughout the meal, stood and said to Coryphee, "You'll make Cindy, here, comfortable in the wagon?"

"Well, I certainly won't leave her out here with you oafs," she said as she slid a thin, burning branch from the fire. "Come on, Lass. Let's find you a place to bed down."

As she climbed the stairs to the wagon's door, Cindy glanced back at the campsite. Driver ducked into the men's tent, and Bard was tapping the ashes out of his pipe into the fire. What caught her attention, though, was Whistler stepping out of the firelight and heading for the edge of the forest.

Probably answering nature's call. I should ask Coryphee about that, she thought, then followed the other woman into the wagon.

The inside was pitch black until Coryphee lit a lantern. In the dim light, Cindy gasped at the array of costumes, props, scenery, and assorted trunks that were stacked to the roof and crammed into every nook and cranny. At the end of a narrow passage through the heaped boxes and traveling theater items, a tapestry hung as a curtain. Coryphee drew it back and she and Cindy passed through into a lady's boudoir.

This is amazing.

The space, which seemed bigger than the wagon that contained it, held a four-poster bed, a vanity with a tall mirror, and an overstuffed chair that looked to be softer than a cloud. The light scent of lavender wafted in the breeze made by the swinging tapestry.

Coryphee hung the lantern on a shepherd's crook.

"All I've got for ya' is this," she said as she uncovered a chaise, which Cindy was sure hadn't been there before, strewn with scarves and a cloak. The plush velvet upholstery, though it fit perfectly with the other furnishings, belied the rough-spun nature of the rest of the troupe.

"Where did that come from? And how does this room fit inside the wagon?"

Coryphee sniffed and shrugged. "It's magic." She held up the heavy cloak. "Ya' can cover y'self with this."

When Cindy took it from her, she saw it was quilted and lined with silk. It was surprisingly light.

Must be stuffed with goose down, she thought.

Coryphee loosened the jerkin that served as a bodice over her shift, then pulled them both over her head in one motion. Cindy blinked hard when she saw Coryphee was naked underneath.

"Close your mouth, Lassie, and don' be shy." She sniffed in Cindy's direction. "Those clothes need an airin'."

Swallowing her embarrassment, Cindy fumbled out of her strange clothes, hung them from a hook on the wall, and climbed into her makeshift bed. The embrace of the chaise and enveloping warmth of the cloak overtook her within a minute.

"Good night, and thanks…" she managed to mutter before her eyes closed of their own volition. A light snore was the only answer she got.

#####

Cindy awoke refreshed, to the sound of whispered voices beyond the tapestry curtain. She only caught snippets of the conversation.

"…still asleep."

"Good…set for tonight."

"You're sure it's safe?"

"…not the first…"

She heard the wagon door close, and a moment later pretended to be asleep as Coryphee parted the curtain.

"Wake up, you," she called. "We're a'leavin' shortly." She tossed a warm biscuit to Cindy when she sat up.

Coryphee pointed to a wash basin and pitcher on the vanity. "Your wash water'll be gettin' cold."

With that she ducked back out through the curtain, leaving Cindy alone.

When she emerged from the wagon, the troupe was busy preparing for departure. Driver tightened Horse's harness while Whistler and Bard folded and stowed their tent on the wagon's roof. Chanteur stood by the dead campfire, idly kicking dirt onto the cold ashes.

Coryphee waved Cindy out of the way as she stitched another satchel of herbs onto the drying cord.

"Make y'self useful," she said and handed Cindy a pouch of blossoms. "Float these in the wash basin. They'll keep the stink of *them,*" she nodded to the men, "outta my space. And empty the chamber pot." Seeing Cindy's lost look, she added, "It's under my bed. If ya havena' used it, ya better. It's a long ride we'll be doin' today."

Suddenly feeling an urgent need, Cindy ducked back into the wagon. A minute later, she emerged, delicately holding the chamber pot at arm's length. Coryphee scrambled to take it from her.

"Lordy, Girl. Ya' shoulda' just pitched it out the window. These oafs know enough to stay clear of it."

Cindy heard chuckles coming from the men but was too embarrassed to look their way.

"We 'bout ready?" Bard called. A chorus of "Aye" from everyone followed. Even Cindy offered one of her own.

"Good. Whistler, up top. Chanteur on the bench with Driver. I'll walk a ways, then we'll switch when I tire." He stopped and looked at Cindy. "Can ya' read palms, Lass?" Cindy just stared. "Tarot cards?" Cindy barely shook her head. Bard nodded and sighed. "Coryphee, dear, could you teach Cindy a few tricks? She can work the crowd while we play, eh?"

Coryphee shrugged and nodded. "Come on in, then. Let's get this over with."

The wagon lurched into motion as the women pushed back the curtain into the boudoir.

"Open the other one," Coryphee said as she propped open the window on one side of the room. Cindy followed her lead with the one opposite. Bathed in the early morning light, the room took on a cheery and airy feel.

Flipping her braid behind her back and tying a silken scarf about her head, Coryphee stepped back through the curtain and returned a moment later with a folding table and chair. She set them up and sat in the chair. Cindy settled onto the chaise.

"Let me see your palm, my dear." The older woman's voice softened into an uncharacteristic soothing and friendly lilt. She drew a finger across the lines on Cindy's palm. "Ah," she whispered, frowning, then her expression brightened, and she grinned when she raised her head and gazed directly into Cindy's eyes.

Cindy, who had never believed in any superstitious nonsense, felt herself drawn into the other woman's sincere smile.

"What do you see?" she asked, breathless.

Coryphee remained silent as she ran her index finger lightly across Cindy's palm, tracing not just the obvious lines, but the mounts and plains, the ridges, and creases. All the while, she kept up a tuneless humming that soothed Cindy and kept her anxiety, but not her skepticism at bay.

Let's see how she does, she thought.

"Very interesting," Coryphee murmured, "and…intriguing." She traced her finger around the edges of Cindy's palm and along each of her fingers. "Fire hands," she said, almost to herself. Coryphee looked up from Cindy's palm with just her eyes, gazing at her through her long lashes. "A passionate soul, then. Likely to get you in trouble, I'd say."

You're telling me, Cindy thought, but promised herself to remain silent, not wanting to give Coryphee any hints.

Coryphee lowered her eyes to Cindy's palm again. Instead of examining the obvious creases, she gently pressed along the base of the fingers, across the palm, and along the bottom of Cindy's hand.

"Jupiter stands for confidence—meh; Saturn is for responsibility—oh, my, yes; Apollo, optimism? Not much there, I'm afraid; Mercury for intelligence." Coryphee met Cindy's eyes with her own. "Very impressive."

First female lead product architect. Not bad.

She stroked the top of Cindy's palm. "Mars. Not aggressive, but not a push-over, either."

I can be a badass when I need to be. Wait, am I buying into this?

Tracing her finger down the side of Cindy's hand, Coryphee continued. "Luna is imagination." She chuckled. "Not surprising *that's* prominent." Next, her finger sensuously circled the bulb of flesh beneath the thumb, sending a thrill through Cindy. "But this. This tells the most about you." Her finger continued its slow circling, and Cindy felt a welcome tingling. "Venus is so…prominent. Romance. Passion. Sex."

Cindy blushed a little. *Nailed that one, too.*

Coryphee smiled knowingly and held up her own hand for Cindy to touch. "Something we have in common, then."

Cindy's breath caught in her throat. "I thought you read the lines."

"Oh, we will, my dear. The lines tell me your past and your future. But the mounds and plains tell me who you are." She returned to Cindy's palm. "For example, I see from your Head Line," she stroked the longest crease running across the palm, "you've al'ays been the smartest, no? And your Life Line shows me you draw strength from others, but don'a really need them, ya think."

Cindy couldn't help but nod. *I know when I'm right, even when others don't.*

"All these things I can tell 'bout ya just from talkin' to ya. This, though," she drew her finger along the length of the deepest crease running along the top of Cindy's palm. "Your Heart Line tells me what you keep hidden inside. Ya fell in love later'n most, but ya fell hard." She touched a point where the line fractured, becoming discontinuous. "An' when it ended, somethin' broke in ya."

Cindy felt tears welling in her eyes. She blinked them away and tried to pull back her hand, but Coryphee's next words stopped her.

"But ya can heal it. Ya can love again."

Her finger hovered over a point where the Heart Line split. One branch quickly faded out to smoothness. The other continued on, growing deeper and stronger until it wrapped around the edge of Cindy's hand.

"Ya get ta decide, Cindy." Coryphee finally raised her head to meet Cindy's eyes. Her face was deadly serious, and her eyes seemed to be filled with compassion. "Ya have one chance, Dear, to find your Way to true love," she drew her finger straight down, crossing a similar branch in her Head, Life, and Fate lines. "That chance will decide ev'rythin'."

How? Did she read my mind?

As if she could, Coryphee said, "It's all written in the lines on your palm."

Cindy swallowed hard. "Teach me," she begged.

Dinner that night was a rabbit, snared, gutted, and skinned by Whistler. It was slim pickings for six of them, but Cindy didn't mind. The day she spent with Coryphee was almost pleasant, the other woman not exactly warming to Cindy's company, but at least becoming tolerant of her. After Coryphee pronounced her "barely able" to read the Head, Heart, and Life lines of her palm, she banished Cindy from the wagon.

I think she just got mad because I nailed her reading, Cindy thought, then smiled as the door slammed behind her.

She then practiced on everyone except Whistler, who steadfastly refused her pleas.

So Chanteur is not the only one with a past to hide.

The long afternoon spent walking alongside Bard behind the wagon in the fresh air sent Cindy straight to sleep after dinner. She stirred but once during the night when whispered voices in the storage part of the wagon briefly woke her, but she quickly forgot that in the warmth of her slumber.

#####

The next day, the path eventually passed out of the forest into a landscape of rolling hills planted with winter wheat, with early spring shoots of beans and barley poking their heads above the fertile earth. Bard and Chanteur joined Whistler atop the wagon, Driver pounded a beat against his seat, and they played songs, some bawdy enough to make Cindy blush, as they wended their way through the fields being tended by the local townsfolk.

Remembering a small drum with a broken head thrown into a dark corner, Cindy retrieved it, took down a string of bells from the side of the wagon, and wove their cord around the rim of the drum. When she joined the men with her homemade tambourine, there were smiles all around, and even a nod of approval from Whistler.

Smiles also accompanied them along their way from the people working the fields. Most stopped their labors, standing and stretching their backs, and clapped along with the beat of the tune. More than one father sent his youngest son running ahead to announce the troupe's arrival.

Their destination revealed itself as they topped a small rise. A few miles ahead, standing proudly atop the highest hill in the verdant valley, stood a small castle. Mist sheathed its dour curtain wall until almost midday. But soon after the young runners arrived, flickering spots of color dotted the grey stones. As they drew closer, Cindy realized brightly colored banners festooned the walls and tiny flags flew from the ramparts.

A crowd was gathering from the surrounding village, and the soldiers and workers from within the walls—blacksmiths, farriers, bakers, and others—lined the approach to the castle gates. Driver pulled Horse to a halt at the brink of the drawbridge, and Chanteur hopped down as an old man approached from inside. He wore a long, embroidered cloak whose hem was badly frayed. A young scribe and a burly guard who wore a doublet adorned with many medals attended him. The old man—the majordomo, Cindy guessed—shuffled forward. His back was bent, and he hobbled with a cane, but when he reached the other end of the drawbridge, he slammed it three times against the wood.

Chanteur drew himself up to his fullest height, swept off his feathered hat, and bowed so deeply that Cindy thought he might tip over.

The old man wheezed, "Who is it that bids entry into Castle Sowich?"

Chanteur bowed again—just his head this time—and said in a booming voice, "We are the Troupe of Songs, bearing gifts of ditties designed to make you dance, hymns to humble the soul, and carols for carousing and cavorting. These gifts we humbly offer to the lord and lady of this fine manor."

The smiles that had broken out on the faces of the guards faded and they shifted their feet uncomfortably at the last. The old man sniffed and sighed.

"The Master has been gone to war these last many years, but Lady Sowich welcomes you to enter and sing for your supper this evening."

Bard, sitting next to Cindy on the wagon whispered, "There hasn't been a war in these parts for nigh on ten years, now."

Chanteur folded his hands in supplication and raised an eyebrow. "Just our supper?"

The old majordomo coughed, then said, "And a bit of coin, as to be judged by the Lady to be fitting and appropriate to her delight."

"Of course, sir. Very good."

As Chanteur bowed again and turned to climb into his place next Driver, Cindy noticed that he and the captain of the guard—the one with all the medals—exchanged a glance, followed by the slightest nod of the captain's head.

"Well, that went well," Chanteur said over his shoulder as the wagon rumbled over the drawbridge.

"Except for the part about being paid as 'fitting and appropriate to her delight,'" Bard muttered.

"Not to worry, I'm sure between Whistler's flute, your mandolin, and my singing," he stressed the last, "Lady Sowich will be transfixed."

Whistler, who had been silent all morning, simply grunted, disparagingly.

"Besides," Chanteur turned in his seat and smiled at Cindy, "Mistress Cindy will earn a few coppers with her newfound palmistry skills, I'm sure."

Not sure whether Chanteur's tone was mocking or serious, Cindy kept silent and felt herself blushing under the man's attention.

#####

The troupe met Lady Sowich late in the afternoon after settling into their quarters in the castle stables. Despite the stench and overall foul nature of their lodgings, Coryphee outfitted Cindy in a seer's costume, complete with a long, layered dress, bandana, copper rings, and bangles. Water infused with wildflower blossoms removed, or at least covered up, Cindy's days-old personal scent.

Lady Sowich sat on a throne set upon a raised dais in the castle's great hall. A squad of guards led them in as if they were prisoners or some delegation from an enemy nation. The majordomo stamped his staff on the ground three times when they were arrayed in a line before the throne and announced them as a troupe of vagabond players. The men all bowed deeply, and Cindy followed Coryphee's lead, curtsying as she had been instructed.

They all raised their heads and looked to the Lady expectantly. She examined each of them with a scowl until her eyes fell upon Chanteur. He bowed again as their eyes met, and the Lady's scowl turned into a look of feral desire. His smile beamed in response.

"Very well," she said to her majordomo, her nose raised in the air. "Arrange a feast for my knights and nobles here in the Great Hall and declare a festival night for the town. Make ready two casks—" the majordomo coughed, "—three casks of middling wine and…four?" he nodded, "sheep for the spit."

"Very good, m'Lady."

A page scurried off toward the kitchen to pass the word.

"And I will meet with a representative of this band to discuss payment."

Bard stepped forward and bowed, but the Lady ignored him and pointed to Chanteur.

"You, there on the end. Attend me."

Without another word, the Lady stood and exited the room through a door behind the throne. Shrugging to Bard, Chanteur followed, smiling widely. Coryphee muttered a curse, spun on her heel, and led the rest of the troupe back to the stables.

#####

Cindy practiced her palm reading skills on Driver and Bard. Whistler simply raised an eyebrow and shook his head when she approached him, and Coryphee claimed she was too busy getting ready for their show. Chanteur reappeared just in time to join the others before they followed their guards into the Great Hall. His doublet was mis-buttoned and one of his boots untied. Coryphee refused to answer his greeting, and Chanteur met Driver's leer with a matching grin and a finger to his lips.

Many of the gathered knights and nobles were well into their cups by the time Cindy and the others marched into the room playing a high-spirited chorale. Coryphee led the way, skipping and twirling, sending her skirts flying. Whistler followed, playing his flute, then Bard with his mandolin and Chanteur belting out the lyrics. Driver and Cindy brought up the rear, him banging on two drums tucked under his arm, and she tapping and shaking her homemade tambourine. They circled the room, weaving among the tables sparsely laden with meats, cheeses, fruit and bread. Serving girls filled empty cups from heavy crockery pitchers.

When the song ended, they stood, again, before the Lady. With sweeping bows and curtsies from the women, the crowd broke into clapping and cries of "Huzzah!"

For the next hour, the troupe played one well-rehearsed song after another. Coryphee danced down the aisles between the tables, evading many grasping hands, and enduring the occasional smack on her backside. Whenever one landed, she held open the pouch tied to her waist into which the offender reluctantly dropped a copper coin.

Bard strolled amongst the tables, also, strumming his mandolin. Women accepted his flirting enthusiastically, though either grudgingly or good naturedly by their male escorts. He knew from experience which to linger over and which to avoid.

Cindy had never seen Whistler so animated. He wore a codpiece under his tight, black hose, a green satin doublet, and a jaunty feathered cap. His flights of tones and trills were matched by leaps that took him high into the air. Landing lightly on one leg, he perched that way and continued playing.

He looks like a stork or a green flamingo, Cindy thought.

Smiling at that mental image, yet impressed by his showmanship, Cindy tried to put on a serious face as she set up her table and chair at the back of the hall close to the door to the stairway that led to the kitchen below. As Coryphee worked the drunken men, their wives and daughters drifted back to Cindy to have their fortunes told. She soon learned, through the meager tips she received, that honesty was not the best policy, regardless of what the lines on the ladies' palms foretold. So, as the night progressed, the ladies' fortunes improved significantly, as did the weight of her coin pouch.

Chanteur's voice rang through the hall, bawdy lyrics slipping easily from his grinning lips. He carried a wondrous cup that, without attention from the serving girls, always remained full. He first shared it with Lady's taster, who nodded his approval and passed it to the Lady. With a nod, from her, Chanteur offered it to the guard Captain, who shook his head with a scowl, and the Majordomo, who continued guzzling it long after it should have emptied.

An ever-filling cup of wine? How? …I know, I know. It's magic.

Chanteur then carried it from table to table as he sang. The deep red of its ever-filling wine, delicious though it was, brought on a heady enthusiasm from the crowd, and coins flowed into the players' pouches almost as freely as the wine from the wondrous cup. As the music drew to a close, so did the eyes of the drunkards, who were all overtaken by a deep slumber.

Many heads lay on the tables, and snores vied with the music in volume, by the time Whistler began the finale. It was a slow ballad, apparently unknown to the other members of the troupe. They looked on in confusion as Whistler strolled amongst the few remaining partygoers who remained awake. The haunting melody brought the guards and servants from other parts of the castle into the hall, and before long, with the help of Chanteur's magical cup, they too soon sat slumped against the wall.

Her own head nodding, though neither she nor any other members of the troupe had partaken of the hypnotic drink, Chanteur's hand on her shoulder startled Cindy awake. With a signal from him, she folded the table and chair and was following the others out of the hall when a signal bell began clanging and an uproar arose from the cellars.

"Alarm! Alarm!" voices echoed up from below. "The treasury 'as been sacked!"

A platoon of guards ran in from the castle yard, blocking the troupe's escape. Their eyes were blurry, but their weapons were sharp. Turning, Cindy found the other end of the corridor they were hurrying down to be blocked by the guard Captain and his men, trapping them between the two squads like flies in amber.

What is going on? What have I gotten myself into?

Lances and pikes poking them from behind forced them down into the dungeons in the deepest bowels of the castle. The guards threw Coryphee and Bard into one cell. Driver, Whistler, and Cindy were shoved into another, but not before the guards snatched from them the women's heavy coin pouches. Purely out of spite, one of the guards ripped Bard's mandolin from his hands and smashed it. Whistler's flute, though, was nowhere to be found when the guards searched him for it.

The guard Captain himself separated Chanteur from the rest of the troupe and dragged him by his hair through another door into the darkness beyond.

Thus began the bleakest night of Cindy's life.

The cell was nothing but four walls of stone with a low doorway closed off by iron bars hung by massive hinges mortared into the stone. Grooves in the door's header and sill eliminated the possibility of escape for even the most emaciated prisoner.

That'll probably be us in a few weeks. I can stand to lose a few pounds, but I wouldn't have picked this diet.

Cindy had no doubt that the supper they sang and danced for all evening would not be forthcoming.

Rough, flat stones made up the cell floor, which was unbroken except for a trough that ran along the back wall to a drain hole in the corner. You couldn't fit a hand down the hole, even if you wanted to. The stench that rose from it made its purpose obvious, though the eyes that reflected the dim torchlight from the hallway belied its use as a highway for the castle's rats.

Driver tried to shake the bars, either to test their strength or simply to rail against the helplessness of their situation. Whatever his motivation, the door barely rattled, and all he did was antagonize the guards, bringing two of them to stand laughing beyond reach outside the door.

Whistler remained silent, as always, but pressed himself against the wall next to the door, out of sight in the shadows.

That guard keeps staring at me. That can't be good.

One guard, fat and middle-aged, whose army uniform had probably never seen a battlefield, leered at Cindy. He licked his lips and said to the much-younger guard, whose own uniform was at least two sizes too big, "Get the key and me pike."

The skinny guard nodded and scurried away.

"If'n you be b'havin' yourselves, now," he said to Driver. "Maybe we'll leave some of 'er for youse."

He looked confused for a moment, then said, "Where be the ladyboy with the whistlin' stick?"

Whistler turned his head toward the corner, as if that would hide him better.

Disgusted, Cindy thought, What a cowar—

Before she could finish her thought, Whistler's voice came from outside the cell.

"I'm in the other cell, you idiot. Please throw her in here when you're done with her."

The guard chuckled, then said in a conspiratorial tone, "Aye, she'll make the rounds."

He grunted again as the skinny guard ran up with a ring of keys in one hand and a six-foot long pike in the other. The pike's long handle was worn smooth, and its head was a rusty spear tip flanked by an axe head on one side and a hooked blade on the other. Although it clearly hadn't been oiled or sharpened in years, to Cindy's untrained eye, it still looked deadly.

Fat Guard snatched the pike from Skinny and told him, "Unlock the door. Quick now, 'afore we get visitors."

Driver raised his hands in submission as the key rattled in the lock and the door's hinges squealed and its iron bars scraped the floor. Whistler, having turned away from the wall, stood poised as if to attack. In a flash, Cindy saw Driver's ineffective door rattling and Whistler's cowardly hiding as the feint-within-a-feint that they were.

"'At's it. Stay back now," Fat Guard said, jabbing the pike at Driver, who stepped back and to the side, leaving Cindy alone in the middle of the cell. She took a step backwards and caught Driver's tiny nod of approval. Whistler had produced his flute from somewhere and held it like a knife.

"Go an' get 'er," Fat Guard said, pushing Skinny into the cell.

As Skinny's second step into the cell landed, Whistler yelled, "Hey!"

The startled guard turned toward the dark corner, only to be met by the end of the flute targeting his eye.

"My eye!" he screamed and dropped to his knees.

Fat Guard reacted exactly according to plan, rushing into the cell, thrusting the pike at the Whistler, who nimbly avoided the thrust and delivered a backhand strike with his flute to the side of Fat Guard's head.

Driver leaped forward and, grabbing the pike just below the head, wrenched it from Fat Guard's hand. Piercing just the fat man's jerkin, he pinned him against the wall with its spear tip. Whistler snatched the key from where Skinny dropped it and gestured for Cindy to follow him out the door. She sidled around behind Driver, then out through the door, where she met the others rushing out of their cell. Whistler held the door open, keys dangling from his hand, grinning widely.

Driver backed out, holding Fat Guard at bay, then slammed the cell door closed. He shook it, checking the lock, then spat in Fat Guard's face.

"Pig," he growled, and followed the others up the steps.

Coryphee led the way, and with very little backtracking the group came to the stables unmolested. Driver held a finger to his lips as he let Horse out of his stall and led him out into the courtyard where their wagon waited. Horse nodded and kept quiet while Driver set about hitching him to the wagon.

For the first time, Cindy had a minute to think about their escape. She glanced sidelong at Whistler.

He's smarter, and braver, than I thought.

Perhaps because he felt her gaze on him, or perhaps because he simply wanted to, Whistler turned to face Cindy. She offered a grudging smile and got a lifted eyebrow and a twitch at the corner of his mouth in response.

Coryphee grabbed Cindy's elbow and signaled her to climb inside, but she paused and looked around. Driver finished harnessing Horse while Whistler climbed onto the bench and Bard onto the roof.

"Where's Chanteur?" Cindy whispered.

She heard muffled curses from above. Coryphee grabbed her arm.

"Get in, Child. He'll find us," she whispered as she dragged Cindy inside.

"Bastard got us into this mess," she heard Driver say as he snapped the reins and the wagon rumbled forward through the deserted castle yard, out through the open gates, and across the drawbridge.

"Where is everybody?" Cindy asked, peering out the back door.

"Sleeping, I suspect, thanks to Chanteur's wondrous cup," Coryphee said, a lilt of laughter in her voice. "Now, shut the door."

Chapter 4

Lady of the Hunt

he troupe's escape was anything but speedy. Strangely, though, there was no pursuit from the castle. There was no sign of Chanteur, either, until they had traveled all night and all the next day. Whistler was cleaning the fish he had entranced with his flute from a small stream nearby when Chanteur walked out of the woods and into the camp.

"Well, that was a debacle," Bard said as Chanteur plopped down on a log next to the campfire. "We got no pay and no supper, and Cindy here nearly got—" He stopped when he saw the look on Cindy's face. "Anyway, we had to scurry out of their like rats in the night. How do you explain that?"

Chanteur seemed genuinely surprised. "Why should I have to explain? They took me unawares as much as you were." He picked a stick from the fire and blew on its glowing tip. A bright flame leapt to life. "It's not my fault that a band of highwaymen used our performance to their advantage."

"Our performance and your magical cup," Whistler growled. "You put everyone to sleep with it."

"Hah! It was your mournful tune that made everyone's eyes droop."

Whistler jumped to his feet the fish knife clutched in his hand.

"Enough!" Coryphee shouted. "We're all here now, safe and no worse off than we were yesterday morning."

Whistler scowled at her, then at Chanteur, before returning his attention to the fish.

"Just hungrier," Driver said as he led Horse to the adjacent field to graze.

"And we have a story to tell around the fire." Chanteur's tone seemed much too jaunty to Cindy's ears, but at least the tension seemed to lessen a bit.

#####

The meager meal they shared passed in silence. When Chanteur leaned back and lit his pipe, he turned to Whistler.

"Plays us a tune, Whistler. Something light and quick."

Whistler scowled in return, then simply stood, and walked away from the fire into the darkness. Chanteur shrugged and turned to Bard.

"A story, then, Bard my friend?"

"Don't feel like it." He crossed his arms defiantly.

Chanteur turned to Cindy, who simply shook her head.

"I've got one," Driver said.

Bard groaned and Coryphee said, "Not too bawdy, Driver. You've ladies present."

That gave Driver pause, but after a moment, he shrugged and began.

"One day, when I was but a wee boy…no, I was more'n a boy, I s'pose. Much more, if ya take me meanin'." He grinned and poked Bard in the ribs. "Anyways, it was early summer, I think. I was mindin' our manor lord's flock o' sheep—"

"Careful, Driver," Coryphee warned.

"Nay, woman. Raise your thoughts from the gutter. I never found the lord's sheep t'be that 'tractive."

Cindy was glad the dim firelight hid her blushing.

"As I was sayin'," Driver continued, "I's watchin' when the sheep suddenly scattered, and a great commotion approached through the wood. Shootin' outta the brush like a arrow loosed from a longbow, a fox tore 'cross the pasture. The little feller had no int'rest in me sheep, not even the lambs who were still sucklin' from the ewes'…

"No, that fox was a'runnin' for 'is life. He darted, full tilt, 'cross the open space, then over the stone wall at the edge of the field." Driver wiggled the fingers of his right hand, mimicking the fox's flight.

"Then, straight 'way behind him come the hounds, hard on 'is scent and bayin' like the end o' the world—which it mighta' been for the fox." All the fingers of Driver's left hand waved furiously as that hand chased the other.

"A moment later, o'course, here come the riders. Our lord led the way followed by his court, his folk letting 'im have the kill. At the back o' the pack rode the only *lady* of the hunt." Driver paused and drank from Chanteur's ever-filling cup, which he had produced, seemingly from nowhere.

Wiping his mouth with the back of his hand, he looked at Cindy, who was intrigued in spite of herself.

"This lady was the lord's youngest, his third daughter—he hadn'a any sons. She had a rep'tation, thanks ta the gossip we hear'd from the manor servants. Headstrong and wild, she was. I know that fo' a fact, as ye shall see."

He glanced to Coryphee, who scowled, but remained silent.

"So, the fox a-darted this a-way, with the hounds in hot pursuit." Driver chased his hands in front of him, again. "The lord and his fellows raced ta keep up."

A third arm and hand seemed to appear following the others. Cindy blinked and shook her head, but when she looked again, Driver had only two.

I must be gettin' tired. Seein' things.

"The hunters tore through there, scattering the sheep ta all corners o' that field. I know'd I'd have a long day collectin' 'em all. All the riders but one jum'd that stone fence and disappeared. All but one o' 'em. That young lass, the lord's daughter, looked my way and stopped short o' the wall. Whether she reined her horse in, or it 'fused to clear the fence, I know not. All's I knows is that she walked that big black stallion to where I lazed about by the fence's gate.

"I scrambled up ta my feet an' tipp'd my cap, tryin' to act the gen'lman, ya know? She simply sat on her high leather throne and give me the once-over. I a'mit I give her the twice-over, if'n you take my meanin'. She'd a-growed inta quite the looker. She'd her pappy's high cheekbones and nose, but her eyes and hair were her mum's. Both blacker'n a moonless night, they were.

"Tippin' my cap again, I mumbled somethin' about the weather, then swung the gate open so she could keep a-huntin'. Instead, tho', she looked to where the pack was dwindlin' away, then slid that finely curv'd leg in her tight breeches over her stallion's haunches and hopped to the ground beside me.

Coryphee sniffed her disapproval at the direction of the story, but when Driver saw Cindy's grin, his own smile broke out and he continued.

"Her black ridin' boots, the heels o' which were sharply poin'd, hugged the curve o' her calves, and her spurs a-jingled as she slowly walked to me."

Driver walked his left hand through the air to where his right stood.

"This high-born lass snapped her ridin' crop 'gainst her boot. The groove there tol' me it weren't the first time she done that. In fac', her next one was like a crack of thunder 'afore the storm. I had a feelin' the storm was a-comin', too."

Cindy chuckled, which deflected Coryphee's protest again.

"Standin' afore me," Driver's hands faced each other knuckle-to-knuckle, "she reached down," his left hand reached out and cupped air, "judgin' the size of my fealty, ya might say."

Coryphee interrupted sharply, "That's enough, Driver—"

But Cindy's barking laugh stopped her mid-protest. Sticking out his tongue to Coryphee, Driver plunged ahead.

"Satisfied by the regard I had for her, she unfurled the banner I was raisin' in her honor, then used that crop o' hers to sink me to me knees."

Seeing Cindy's blush in the firelight and Coryphee's hint of a smile, Driver drove the rest of his story home.

"For the next little while, th' lass taught that young buck—an' this old sod truth be told—a thin' or two." He shook his head, and a smile touched his lips in remembrance.

"At long last, I bit down on the ridin' crop that she held in my teeth like a horse's bit. I know my choppers left a mark because I was a-pickin' splinters from my teeth for days."

The rest of the troupe, who sat in rapt silence throughout Driver's recitation, with the occasional snorts of laughter or mumbled encouragement, broke into loud laughter.

"Then, with what looked to be practiced ease, she dressed in a moment and I, still wavin' my flag in the breeze—but wit' no gale to keep it flyin' at that poin'—I boosted her into her stirrups. With a truly evil smile, she held her leather-bound foot out fer me ta kiss. Which, given the recen' activities, I was glad ta 'blige, just to see her gone."

Thinking the story was over, Cindy clapped her hands. But Driver held up a finger and continued.

"Word come down from the manor servants in the early fall that the young lady was bein' sent off ta a convent as her prospects for marriage were ruined. I packed up 'at night and skipped out just ahead o' the lord's sergeant and 'is men."

Cindy's mouth hung open as realization struck. "So, you have a child?"

Driver shrugged and his face lost all trace of humor. "Tha's what they say. I'll never know fer sure. I know I wasn'a her first, and I doubt I was her last."

By this time, the fire had died down to dull embers. Their glow cast a reddish light that served only to illuminate the deep sadness on Driver's face.

Bard clapped him on the shoulder and said, "Well told, old friend. You'll be takin' my job soon."

With the tension eased, the men, except Whistler, who had reappeared from the forest during Driver's story, rose and headed for their tent. Cindy's eyes followed them as they walked away, joking quietly.

This troupe is deeper than I would have guessed. Chanteur gets away, then reappears a day later no worse for wear, and no one is surprised or even asks him about it, least of all Coryphee. Driver seems able to talk to Horse, and Bard can tell many-layered tales of these woods. And Whistler. What about Whistler? Where does he wander off to most every night? Why does he keep so silent, and just seem to watch? Well, he watches until needed, like when we were in the cell, then uses his flute as a weapon! And I'm not sure which was more hypnotic, Chanteur's Wonder Cup or Whistler's flute?

I know which of the two is more interesting, and which is more dangerous.

"Come on, Girlie. There'll be no sleeping in tomorrow." Coryphee stood at the base of the steps leading up into the wagon.

"In a minute," Cindy said without looking. Her focus was on Whistler, who stood next to the fire, absently kicking dirt onto the embers.

"Why so sad," she said as she approached.

He startled a little, as if he had forgotten where he was, or didn't realize he wasn't alone.

"Oh, I don't know. Just…" He shrugged.

"Where do you wander off to every night?"

He bristled a little. "Just clearing my head," he said and turned for the safety of the tent, but Cindy laid a hand on his arm to stop him.

"You always look depressed after you 'clear your head.' You look like it's more muddled, not clearer. Maybe you should just stay here and have a laugh with your friends."

He took her hand in his and looked deeply into her eyes. "Are you my friend?"

Her breath caught in her throat. "I…want to be. A friend. At least to you." He lifted an eyebrow. "And the others."

He dropped his gaze, squeezed her hand, then strode to the tent without another word.

And he's the deepest of them all, she thought as she watched him go.

#####

During the night, Cindy awoke from a dream where she stood at the brink of an impossibly deep crevasse in the ground. On the other side stood Chanteur, beckoning for her to take a running start and leap over. In the far distance, though, Whistler stood on a bridge spanning the chasm. He simply stood looking in her direction, neither encouraging nor discouraging her choice.

Whispers outside the window brought her to wakefulness, and she recognized Chanteur and Coryphee in another of their late-night trysts. Pulling the blanket up to her chin, Cindy was just about to resume her dream when the sound of a palm striking a cheek brought her fully awake. Coryphee appeared at the curtain a few moments later, but Cindy was already feigning sleep, eyes open to slits.

Tiptoeing, Coryphee opened a trunk in which she kept her clothes and slipped a heavy leather bag into it. The contents made a distinctive clinking sound as they settled into place.

Chapter 5

May Day

The wagon bumped along the forest road all morning, while Coryphee showed Cindy how to weave wildflowers into crowns for each of them and garlands for the wagon. In late afternoon, when they arrived at a good-sized village, they set up a stage on the edge of the village green. Over the stage, the men unfurled a canvas awning, which the women decorated with their strands of white and yellow spring flowers. In the center of the green, the village's men stacked wood for a bonfire, while their wives and daughters strewed bright flowers everywhere.

"What are we celebrating," Cindy asked Coryphee as they laid out brightly colored costumes for the troupe.

"'Tis Beltane, Dearie. Start of summer. Tomorrow, the town's cattle go to the high pastures and summer planting starts. Tonight, though, we celebrate the slumber of Old Man Winter and the awakening of his sister Maiden Summer. Don' be surprised ta see Whistler's pipe bring the fairies outta their hidin' spots into the light."

"I'll certainly do my best," Whistler said as he joined them in the wagon. "Your tambor—er, that bell drum you fashioned—will help, I'll warrant."

A flush of pride swept over Cindy at his praise before she thought, *He almost said 'tambourine,' but I don't think I ever called it that. How does he know that word, and why stop himself from using it?*

"'Ndeed," Coryphee added. "You can lead the cattle with it." She looked pointedly at Whistler. "Somebody needs ta teach ya the steps first, though."

Taking the hint, Whistler took Cindy's hand and walked past where Driver led Horse, who wore his own garland, in a loop around the green as the village children queued up to ride on his wide back. Some offered an egg or strip of jerky, while others could only recite a poem of blessing in payment. All were welcome, with no payment sought, yet freely given. Horse seemed to enjoy the attention, snorting, and whinnying as the youngsters grabbed his mane and squealed with delight when he tossed his enormous head in response.

"We'll have tasty breakfasts for the next few days," Whistler whispered as they passed and left the green through a gap in the surrounding buildings. "Especially tasty since the fixings were freely offered and gladly accepted."

Impressed, she thought, *This guy's like a mountain pool. Calm on the surface, but with currents running deep.*

Wait—where'd that analogy come from? And why am I still holding hands with him?

Refusing to admit to herself how natural and comfortable his hand felt in hers, she gave it a little shake to break their contact. Whistler's shoulders slumped as their hands parted. Cindy felt a chill as a cold wind blew between the small, but well-kept, houses.

Behind the garden at the back of the house, a path led down to the winter pastures. Whistler stopped there and played a phrase on his flute while he tapped first one foot, then the other, in a complex pattern in time to the music. After watching the sequence twice through, Cindy imitated his steps, making only one or two mistakes.

I guess those years of ballet and tap lessons were actually worth something.

When she had those steps down, Whistler changed it up and added twirls, hops, and skips. Feeling the music as much as she heard it, Cindy anticipated these additions and picked them up naturally.

They practiced until the light faded with the setting sun. Whistler stopped playing and cocked his head to listen. On the breeze, Cindy heard the lowing of cows as the village boys drove them up from the winter pastures toward the village.

"Perfect timing," Whistler said with the biggest smile Cindy had seen on his face. "You ready?"

Cindy matched his smile and nodded enthusiastically.

"Good." His eyes flashed as she reached out and took his hand again. Together, they met the line of boys driving the cows up the path and Whistler, reluctantly letting go of Cindy's hand, took up the tune. Feeling as if she had done this her whole life, Cindy danced at the head of the procession into the heart of the village.

The bonfire came to life and the villagers lining the narrow street joined the procession, picking up Cindy's dance and laughing with delight as she threw in her own flourishes. Bard strummed his mandolin and Chanteur added his voice, singing lyrics intended to bring out the magical denizens of the wood.

Cindy slowly led the village around the roaring fire three times before Whistler played a long note that sank from the bright, playful tune into a quiet, soothing melody. The villagers encircled the bonfire and joined hands, adding their voices to Chanteur's. They sang a lullaby meant to lull Winter into his summer slumber.

When Whistler's last notes' echoes faded into the night, cheers and applause broke out from all the adults gathered. The children made a beeline for the tables laid with cakes, pies, and all manner of sweets.

Flushed and short of breath, Cindy accepted embraces from the townsfolk, who whispered their thanks with words of "best Beltane, yet" and "you've ensured a fine harvest." When the last of them had gone to join and rein in the children stuffing their faces, Bard took both her hands in his.

"Welcome to our troupe," he said with a note of seriousness she had not heard from him before.

"Hear, hear!" Driver called and nudged Bard out of the way so he could lift Cindy off her feet in a great bearhug. "Aye, you're one o' us now," he bellowed.

"'Ndeed," Coryphee said when Driver set Cindy back on her feet. "I coudna' done't better myself." Cindy failed to notice the hint of jealousy in Coryphee's voice, though.

Whistler reached for her hand, but Chanteur stepped in and took Cindy in his arms. Pressed against him, she slipped her own arms around his neck, almost against her will.

"The festivities are just getting started," he whispered. "I'll look for you later."

Stepping back, but keeping an arm possessively around Cindy's waist, he said, "Come on, let's eat before it's all gone, then we'll give them one hell of a party!"

#####

The full moon had climbed high in the sky and started its slide toward morning before the music stopped and couples stumbled back to their homes arm in arm or, just as often, with lips pressed to each other's and hands wandering to leather laces.

It was easy to blame Chanteur's wondrous cup since that evening it dispensed desire rather than drowsiness, but his singing and the music, led by Whistler's flute, were just as powerfully seductive. Cindy and Coryphee led the dances, each becoming wilder and more sensuous. More than once, a trill from Whistler, a thumping of Driver's drum, or a rattle of Cindy's tambourine rescued one or the other from being pulled into some horny lap.

At long last, only embers remained of the bonfire, and youths proved their bravery by leaping over them. Cindy, exhausted, sat upon a log beyond the embers' faint glow. Feeling hands on her shoulders, she leaned back into the soothing massage.

"That feels good," she murmured to no response. The fingers dug deep into her tight muscles, then moved to the sinews of her neck. The exertions of the celebration drained from her under the hands' ministrations, leaving her stuporous until something snapped her back to reality.

What the heck?!?

Another pair of hands kneaded the small of her back, while yet another slid up the sides of her ribs.

"Hey!" she barked as she jumped to her feet and spun around, expecting to find leering men. Instead, she stared into the emptiness of the night. But it wasn't fully empty. Black shapes darted about her, distinguished from the night, not by color, but by how they made the world waver in their wakes.

Cindy stood frozen in place while the wisps flew like leaves in a gale about her, passing just close enough to drag coldness across her belly or breast. She felt a wind blow back her hair and press her shift tight against her body. She looked back for the safety of the bonfire and village but found herself surrounded by trees.

I can't move. So how did I get into the forest?

Terror and panic flooded her thoughts, but her body refused to move to her command. Ethereal fingers became hands grasping and stroking. Hands became arms wrapping about her with a frozen embrace. One locked her voice in her throat before she could call out. Another, pressed to her chest then reached in to touch her pounding heart.

A calmness suddenly replaced her terror as the sound of a hazel staff slamming the ground reverberated through the wood. A brilliant flash from behind loosened the wood spirits' grip on her soul and drove them back into the surrounding trees. Freed from their deadly embrace, Cindy turned to find Jack Green standing in the glow of his staff.

"Thank you, Mr. Green," she whispered, catching her breath. "What happened?"

Jack cast the light from his staff further into the forest, and Cindy saw those slithering figures slink back into the dark.

"This night, Beltane, thins the veil 'tween worlds, Child. Ancient spirits like these," he threw his light wider yet, sending dark forms scurrying, "can cross over and possess ya if ya not careful. Best to stay within the fire's glow this night."

He nodded for her to follow as he wove his way out of the forest.

"Needing you to save me has become a habit, I'm afraid. But I'm still lost here with no idea how to get home."

Jack just shook his head and stopped at the edge of the village's pasture.

"I gave you the best advice I can, my Dear."

Cindy opened her mouth to protest, to tell him that "through her heart" was not a direction she knew, when voices calling her name echoed across the field. Jack nodded farewell and, turning back to the woods, extinguished his light.

"Will I see you again," Cindy whispered, somehow knowing to keep their encounters private.

Jack stopped mid-stride and turned back to look over his shoulder, then simply shrugged and hurried into the darkness of the trees as the voices calling across the field drew closer. Whistler's was closest, calling her "Cynthia."

"I'm here," she called back starting toward his welcome voice, but thought, *When did I tell him my real name?*

Before their hurried steps brought them together, though, Chanteur ran in from the dark and swept Cindy off her feet.

"Thank the gods we found you," he said, then shouted, "I've found her."

"But Whistler," she said before she felt Chanteur's lips pressed to hers. Stiffening at first, then slowly melting into his arms, her fears of the night washed away. When she snaked her arms around his neck, he lifted her and carried her back to their camp, brushing past Whistler on the way.

Chapter 6

Spring's Rare Delights

mid the relieved greetings of the troupe, Chanteur set Cindy on her feet. With belated warnings to "be careful" and "don'a go wand'rin' off," Driver and Bard ducked into the tent and Coryphee climbed the steps into the wagon.

At the top, she waited for Cindy, but Chanteur lifted his cup and said, "Give us a moment, please."

Coryphee scowled and threw Cindy daggers from her eyes but turned without a word of protest and slammed the wagon door behind her. Whistler, a look of disappointment on his face, simply shook his head and strode off to wherever he went every night.

Run away like you always do. Cindy's thoughts felt fuzzy. *At least Chanteur knows what he wants. And so do I.* She pulled Chanteur's head to hers until their parted lips met.

Feeling the warmth of their kiss coursing through her veins, she gladly matched the long draught he took from the cup with one of her own. Her mind foggy, she followed as he took her by the hand and ran along the path the cattle had earlier followed to the high pastures.

An hour of hiking and more than a few stops to sip from the never-empty cup later, the two reached a wide meadow on the slope between two mountain peaks that overlooked the town. Amid the wild daffodils, Chanteur took Cindy in his arms and, without pretext or resistance, pulled her down into the soft grass.

#####

The sun was already high in the sky when Cindy awoke. Alone. Shivering and naked beneath the blanket of her thin shift, she raised her head to see her only companions were several cows munching on the sweet grass, bees buzzing among the wildflowers, and one boy from the village watching her from across the field.

Slipping on her meager garments, she looked about for any sign of Chanteur and tried to recall the events of the previous night. A small smile touched her lips as flashes of memory returned to her, but when she pieced together the fragments enough to remember what she did and allowed to be done here in the high meadow, she recoiled in shame.

What were you thinking? You weren't. That's the problem. Now you may have an even bigger burden to carry. And where is that bastard?

Chanteur was long gone, as she feared the rest of the troupe was, as well. Her fears were confirmed when she finally found her way back to the village. The green was a bustle of activity, but the troupe's wagon and all its members were nowhere to be found.

"I wondered when ya'd turn up," a female voice called from the door of the village's only tavern. "He said ya'd be lookin' for a job."

Cindy blinked in confusion, recognizing the tavern's owner, Ruby, from the night before. Confused, she asked, "Who told you that?"

"Why, the singin' stud, o' course."

Cindy thought for a moment. *The bastards left me here alone with no money. And no way home.*

"What kind of job?"

The woman snorted a derisive laugh. "I got an empty whore's bed I need ta fill."

"I'm no whore."

"'At's not what the singin' stud said." Ruby laughed again as she turned back to enter the tavern. "Take it or not. I don'a care."

Cindy stood in the village street, nervously looking around at the hustle and bustle of the market.

There's got to be some job besides whoring I can get—

"What!?!" Ruby's voice shrieked from inside the tavern. "I jus' hired ya yes'rday! Then begone wit' ya."

A buxom young woman, the tavern's serving girl, and an even younger looking man tumbled through the tavern's door hand in hand. A crockery mug flew after them, passing between their heads. The mug landed with a thump at Cindy's feet.

The two lovers laughed as they hurried out of range. Ruby appeared in the doorway, hands on her hips. Cindy looked down at the mug, then picked it up and held it out to her.

"Seems you have another opening," she said with the hint of a smile. "I can sling ale as well as *she* did."

Ruby eyed her suspiciously. "But fer how long will ya be stickin' 'round?"

Cindy shrugged. "Longer than she did."

Ruby grunted. "Get yer butt in here, then."

She turned her back and Cindy followed her inside.

Chapter 7

Bells of Summer

Cindy's stint as a waitress in that off-campus bar back in college served her well over the next few weeks. Fending off customers' wandering hands with a slap and a laugh or giving back equally rude comments came naturally to her. Though she wouldn't admit it, Cindy figured Ruby appreciated her ability to keep the room's mood festive, which kept the customers drinking instead of fighting. Partly it was the way she sang Bard's songs as she danced between tables carrying mugs of ale. But mostly it was because she fit right in, and even seemed to dictate the spirit of the place.

Under her lighthearted attitude and laughing banter, though, a deep-seated anger seethed. Her anger had many targets: Pops for laying a trap with his creepy music; Chanteur, of course, for seducing, then abandoning her; and the rest of the troupe for leaving her to fend for herself. But mostly, she raged against her own stupidity.

As soon as I have enough coin, I will find those double-crossing bastards. Then…oh, then…

Every waking moment, when she wasn't wearing her jovial barmaid persona, thoughts of how she could extract her revenge provided fodder for her daydreams and her nightmares.

Cut his balls off... Burn that rattle-trap wagon, using Bard's new mandolin for kindling... With Cory-bitch inside... Steal Horse... And break that stupid flute over Whistler's head.

#####

After two, then three weeks passed from her night on the green velvet of the upper pasture without her monthly period, Cindy fell into an edgy sulk. The mood in the tavern followed suit.

"Ya're not so 'appy these days," Ruby said one night after they had rousted everyone out of the tavern. "'Tis hurtin' bus'ness."

Cindy wouldn't meet her eye. "I got a load on m'mind."

"Me thinks yer carryin' yer load lower down then yer head. Like way down in yer…heart."

It's lower than that, she thought.

But, when her blood returned a month later, the tavern's patrons raised their mugs in celebration, though they had no idea what they were celebrating.

That morning, after they scrubbed the bar, tables, and floor, Ruby had her suspicions about Cindy's mood swings confirmed when Cindy insisted on doing her own laundry.

"So, ya be free o' him, now, eh?"

Cindy tried to hide her surprise behind a blank expression. She couldn't meet Ruby's eyes, but just nodded.

"I 'spect ya'd be wantin' to light out, now."

Cindy hadn't thought past her next meal in weeks. Realization of why she stayed in that godforsaken village broke through the clouds that had cloaked her mind these last weeks.

I wanted to make sure my child would have a home.

That thought had never occurred to her before.

Why am I still here? Now, especially, I have no ties here.

The tears came in a torrent. Her celebratory mood twisted inside her into a pit of grief and she sank down onto a bench.

It's for the best, Dear One. This is no place to bring you into the world, and I'd be no good mother for you.

Although she believed the first to be true, she knew in her heart the last part was a lie.

Ruby watched Cindy's face collapse into a mess of tears and snot, then sighed. Without a word, she went into her rooms at the back of the tavern and returned with a clean damp rag, a small pouch, and a leather pack cinched at the top with a thong and sealed with wax.

She handed the rag to Cindy. "Clean y'self up, Lass. Ya look a wreck."

Cindy half smiled her thanks and wiped her eyes and nose. Ruby hefted the pack and plunked it on the table in front of Cindy.

"Here ya be. He lef' 'is for ya afore…"

"Chanteur?"

Ruby's laugh dripped contempt. "The singin' ass? Nay, Girl, 'twas the quiet one with the whistlin' pipe."

"Whistler?" Cindy felt her heart skip a beat, then eyed Ruby sharply, anger flaring in her voice. "Why now? Why wait so long to give this to me?"

Ruby, unfazed by Cindy's stare, just shrugged. "I fig'red ya weren't ready ta go nowhere…'til now."

Her anger at Ruby, who had helped her in her own rough-edged way, melted away and Cindy turned her attention to the bag, prying the wax seal from the knot and opening it. She pulled out her traveling clothes, the breeches, boots, and jerkin she started this strange adventure wearing. Beneath them was a money pouch that felt heavy when she lifted it. When it was halfway out of the pack, she thought better of removing it altogether and set it quietly back down.

The last item was a note written on rough paper in a beautiful flowing hand.

"Ya ken read 'at?" Ruby asked and looked surprised when Cindy nodded.

Written in perfect English, the note read,

"Cynthia,

"First, I am so sorry that Chanteur took advantage of you last night."

I hate to tell you, Whistler, but I was a willing participant.

"He can command his magic cup to fill with many different potions, including ones that heighten desire, lower inhibitions, and encourage forgetfulness. I fear you fell victim to just such an elixir."

Well, that would explain a lot. Her memories of that night were still decidedly fuzzy.

"Second, I am even more sorry that we—no, I—have left you to fend for yourself in this strange world. I trust that if you are reading this, Ruby has fulfilled her half of our bargain. The money left for you is both your and my share of our Beltane pay. It should be enough for you to find your Way Home. Remember that your Way lies through your heart."

Wait. That's what Jack Green said. How does he know that?

"Finally, you should know that not all of us agreed with the decision to leave you behind. I certainly did not, and neither did Bard. Horse even refuses to budge, although Driver is talking to him as I write this. Chanteur, can't wait to run, and Coryphee, though she won't even talk to Chanteur, is frankly, glad to be rid of you."

That's no surprise.

"For my part, I have no one and nowhere else to go. I tell you all of this so you know how sorry I am, and to remind you that your heart will lead you, if you let it. If your Way passes my way again—"

That's it?

The note ended abruptly, and in her mind's eye, Cindy saw Whistler shoving the paper into the pack and sealing it quickly before handing it to Ruby for safekeeping as the troupe's wagon rumbled out of the village.

Cindy turned to Ruby who still hovered over her. "Where would they be now?"

Ruby shrugged. "Who ken say? They's a wand'rers."

"Come on, Ruby, you know more than you're telling."

The other woman sniffed. "Aye, but ya's best rid o' 'em."

Cindy's voice went cold. "Oh, trust me, I don't want to rejoin them. I want my justice."

They locked eyes for a few heartbeats, then Ruby nodded and handed over the pouch she still held. It contained a loaf of bread and a smoked haunch of some small animal.

"Aye, they deserve that." She stepped forward and placed a hand on Cindy's shoulder. "The sun's high in the sky, which means solstice celebration'll be soon. 'ey'll be callin' the tune for 'em what dance an' worship the sun and moon."

Druids?

"Where can I find them?"

"Up the summer pasture—ya should know 'at way," Ruby grinned, and Cindy nodded ruefully. "Then climb through the pass 'tween the two peaks. Once through, y'll see a high valley with a circle o' standin' stones. 'At's where they'll be."

Cindy stood and to her surprise, she pulled Ruby into a warm hug.

"Thank you for looking after me these last weeks."

Ruby wiped a tear from her eye, then snorted. "Hell, now I gotta find me 'nother wench."

They both laughed and embraced again.

#####

The climb through the mountain pass was steep and took Cindy two days. Auntie Hemlock provided shelter, and on the morning of the third day, feeling very alone, Cindy called for a friend.

"Jack? Jack, if you can hear me, I really need your advice."

Auntie Hemlock swayed her branches, perhaps disapprovingly, but also perhaps as a warning. When Cindy called out his name, louder this time, the lowest branches behind Cindy parted and Jack Green hobbled into the dark space beneath them.

"What is it this time?" His voice croaked.

Cindy immediately knew her mistake. Jack's bald pate was uncovered, and the branches and leaves that made up his long hair fell in tangles about his shoulders. On his feet he wore, not his rough leather boots with pointed toes, but soft slippers, and his belly no longer lapped over his belt.

"Did I…waken you?"

"O' course ya did, Missy! It's nigh on summer. I was sound 'sleep in my warm bed 'neath the holly oaks." Jack's voice, which began as a rough growl, settled into a resigned sigh. "What do ya need?"

Cindy, feeling embarrassed that she disturbed his slumber, looked down at her fingers fidgeting in her lap.

"I…I…" She stopped and gathered her thoughts. "When you told me my way home was through my heart, at first I was confused." She frowned. Talking about her feelings had never been easy. "I've always followed my head, not my heart. What's the best move to advance my career? Who should I date, or worse, who should I marry who can give me the most? Whether that's dinners, gifts, trips, or…sex." Jack raised a single eyebrow making Cindy blush. "It's true. My misadventure in the high pasture was as much my doing as Chanteur's. I thought he could give me the most in this world. I wasn't even thinking whether he could get me home. I guess my old habits took over."

Cindy paused to swallow the lump that rose in her throat. She blinked away the tears that threatened to burst out. Jack simply stood there, quietly leaning on his staff.

"I guess what I'm trying to say is that I don't know how to follow my heart. I never have."

At last, she couldn't hold back the tears any longer. They left salty trails through the grime on Cindy's cheeks as her shoulders shook in time with her sobs. Jack stood passively, letting her cry for a minute while Auntie Hemlock swished her branches in sympathy. But when she reached her branches down to give Cindy a hug, he tapped his staff on the ground and shook his head.

"Well, 'at's a sad tale," he said with a tinge of sarcasm. "But it won'a help ya git home, now, will it? 'Twas your mind 'at brought ya here. Forty minutes o' yer time, wasn't it?"

"Wait, how do you know—"

He waved his hand dismissively and yawned. "'Tis magic. But 'tain't yer mind 'at'll take ya back." He placed his free hand on her shoulder and his voice softened. "Open yer 'eart. Listen to what it's been tryin' ta tell ya. Only then can ya foller it home—wherever *home* may be."

He patted her shoulder twice, gave her a wink, then turned on his heel and nodded to Auntie Hemlock. She took her cue and wrapped Cindy in her embrace.

"Thank you," Cindy called as Jack stepped out through the branches.

He simply raised his hand in response and was gone.

#####

The valley laid out before her was beautiful. From her vantage point at the crest of the mountain pass, she could see the circle of standing stones Ruby told her about. They stood on a rise that commanded the surrounding terrain. The stream with which she shared the gap between the mountains flowed in a straight line down the slope toward the valley. Still heavy with snowmelt, it became a torrent which dropped to the valley floor in a spectacular waterfall. The mist it conjured obscured the lower reaches of the mountainside.

Beyond, though, Cindy saw the river split into a moat that encircled six other concentric henges—circles of ditches, earthen mounds, stonewalls, wooden posts and finally, at the center, seven giant monoliths set in their own tight circle and crowned with equally massive lintel stones.

It's like Stonehenge, except it's alive.

Beyond the ceremonial space, a thick, dark forest filled the rest of the valley.

Bridges crossed the river at the four points of the compass, with matching gaps in the interior henges. The innermost had gates that stood open. Within the outermost circle, bounded by the river, orchards of apple, pear, cherry, and chestnut trees were in full blossom. The riot of color belied the orderliness of their ranks. Bare earth mounds with freshly planted seedlings sprouting from them revealed the orchard's true nature. The trees stood as living grave markers feeding the generations that followed.

The next ring inward held an encampment. Campfires sent lazy trails of smoke into the air amid tents of all description. Brightly colored banners and streamers flicked in the light breeze. At the far side, Cindy could see the troupe's wagon through the smoky haze.

I'll hide among the camps until I can circle around to the forest. Then, when it gets dark, I'll light my own sacrificial fire right under that damned wagon.

Continuing her survey, she saw sharply pointed markers that rose in various places within the smaller interior rings. Two of them, one to the east of the center and one to the west, had garlands of wildflowers draped over them. At the very center of the innermost ring, an altar made by a flat stone on top of two perfectly round ones, flashed golden in the sunlight. Heaped on and around it were mounds of every kind of tool, baskets of farm produce, shields and weapons, and gold. Lots of gold. Piles of gold crowns, bracelets, necklaces, and even a golden breastplate awaited.

They waited for tomorrow, on the solstice, when the rising and setting sun would bless these prized possessions of both the rich and the poor.

All these things Cindy saw and understood with a clarity that was beyond human ability.

How do I know this? Somebody wants me to understand, but why?.

That notion sent a chill down her spine, but also offered some comfort that perhaps her heart was leading her down the correct path. Bringing her back to reality, her stomach, empty since the day before when she had finished Ruby's provisions, growled.

The correct path right now is this steep trail that winds back and forth down the mountain to where I might find a meal.

#####

When she reached the valley floor, Cindy joined a group of pilgrims headed for the encampment. She easily fell in step with a young family in charge of a two-wheeled cart that held the groups offerings and supplies. The father led an old sway-backed horse, while the mother kept her eye on their two sons and a daughter, all below the age of ten. Their smiling faces and the children's playfulness raised Cindy's spirits, and she happily lent a hand whenever the cart bogged down in a muddy spot and needed a push.

After they rattled across a bridge over the muddy river, the group stopped and began apportioning out food from inside the cart. Cindy, who had nothing to share, turned to walk further inward when the daughter, a young girl with straw-colored hair and freckles, tugged on her sleeve.

"Won't you join us?" she asked and held out a bundle wrapped in a rough spun cloth.

Cindy looked up from the child's smiling face to her mother, who wore her own smile and nodded.

"Thank you," she said, swallowing the lump in her throat and gently taking the bundle from the girl. "I would love to."

"Good," said the girl's father. "I'm hungry."

The family, including Cindy, all laughed, and she felt her own stomach growl again, even louder this time, which made the girl burst into giggles.

Over the meager, but hearty, meal, Cindy discreetly asked about the troupe.

"Aye, they come ev'ry year," the father said.

"You have a festival, then?" Cindy asked.

"Aft'wards," the mother said. "Firs' they lead the blessin's an' chants an' such."

"They're part of the ceremony?"

"Ayuh. Without 'em there'd be no wakin' the goodly spirits," she said.

"Nor scarin' away the bad 'uns," the father finished.

This news gave Cindy pause.

If I burn the troupe tonight, these poor people will suffer—whether because the blessing ceremony will be ruined, or because they think it will be. Either way, this whole community will worry about the weather and the harvest and the winter to come.

The children squealed with delight when their mother broke apart a sweet bread filled with strawberries. Cindy felt her mouth water when they handed her a piece.

I suppose I could wait until after *the festival.*

#####

As night fell, Cindy made her way around the encampment to the entrance closest to the troupe's wagon. With no tent, and not wanting to impose further on her temporarily adoptive family, she slipped across the bridge and followed a well-worn path to the edge of the forest that stood a few hundred yards to the north.

Settling in for a night in Auntie Hemlock's embrace, wiped out by the day's travels, and with a full belly for the first time in days, Cindy was drifting into a blissful sleep when the sound of footsteps on the path next to her tree snapped her awake. Parting the branches, she saw in the light of the full moon, a familiar figure plodding along. When he was ten paces into the woods, he looked around guiltily, then blew a few notes on his flute. A silvery light popped into being above his head and cast a glow out to several paces in front of him. With its light to guide him, Whistler plunged into the woods.

Despite her weariness, and now wide awake with adrenaline, Cindy followed, careful to watch where she placed her feet and stepping only in time with Whistler's stride. When the glow of the campfires and the echoes of voices had faded, Whistler left the path and followed a game trail through the thick undergrowth.

Dropping back to where she was following the glow of his light rather than Whistler himself, Cindy worked her way along as quietly as she could. Twice, though, when a branch hidden below the forest loam snapped beneath her foot, Whistler stopped and listened for a minute before continuing. Luckily, many forest creatures were still active or just coming awake. The squirrels' scratching as their claws gripped the trees' bark, along with the flutter of swallows and bats as they hunted buzzing insects, covered Cindy's progress.

She began to feel strange as she followed Whistler through the darkness. The thick canopy above blocked most of the moonlight, so she could focus only on the light bobbing along ahead and the treacherous trail below. Waves of disorientation swept over her and more than once she had to stop and get her bearings as the surrounding forest seemed to change with every step.

Gone were the rough trunks of pine and fir trees, to be replaced by thick, heavy oaks, beech, and ash trees. Her nose tickled and threatened to sneeze, for the clean, clear air took on a modern, industrial tinge.

Her head felt like the worst hangover from her college days by the time Whistler's light stopped advancing and blinked out. Cindy could see little details, but it appeared he stood on the edge of a clearing. Faint artificial yellow light glowed in the open space beyond. He stood stock still, his posture rigid, yet focused.

He's watching something. Waiting for something or someone. What is he looking at?

Cindy resisted the urge to sneak forward, knowing that the slightest sound would break the frozen tableau and expose her.

After several minutes, Whistler's shoulders slumped, and he moved sideways, back into the forest. Hurrying to follow, Cindy fell to her knees as the waves of disorientation swept over her again and again. Pain and nausea held her in place until Whistler's flute tweeted off to her right and his guiding light blinked back to life. Desperately, she stepped off the trail and stumbled through the undergrowth oblivious to the commotion she was causing.

When she found the new game trail that Whistler was following, she fell into step behind him and the pain in her head and the sickness in her belly eased.

Several more minutes of trudging through the forest followed, then again, Whistler's light went out. The trees had thinned out enough that they could proceed by the light of the moon, now high in the sky. The sounds of the forest creatures covered the sound of Whistler's passing as well as Cindy's. So it was that she was almost upon him before she realized he had stopped at the edge of another clearing. Two hooded figures stood in the glade, murmuring. The words were indistinct, but the voices were clearly recognizable to Cindy. Chanteur and the Guard Captain laughed as they shook hands, and Chanteur raised his voice enough for Cindy to hear him clearly.

"…more gold 'an ya can carry!"

The two conspirators parted, melting into the woods.

"We have to stop them," Whistler whispered from right behind Cindy.

She nearly jumped out of her skin.

"Jeez! You scared the crap out of me."

Although she couldn't see his face, she heard his smile. "And here I thought that stink was just you."

Her precisely aimed elbow caught him in the side. "Is that how you knew I was here," she joked.

"No, but you sounded like a tornado sneaking along behind me."

A tornado? Here? Wherever here is.

"They're going to steal the blessings, aren't they?"

"They're going to *try* to. But they won't if we play our cards right."

"How?"

"I have a plan."

Whistler eyed her clothes and said, "I see you got the go-bag I left for you. I meant what I said in the note. I'm truly sorry I abandoned you. I…I've been lost for a long time. I thought you might help me find my Way, but then you went off with Chanteur." He shrugged. "I was angry, I guess."

Cindy's plan for revenge evaporated before her mind's eye.

Did he say, 'The Way' with a capital 'W'?

Before she could ask, he added, "By the way, what took you so long to catch up?"

Memories of her lost baby came flooding back, along with her motivation for revenge. She just shook her head in response. Care for her newfound friends, the young family, softened her desire for revenge, though, and focused it on just one member of the troupe. The "Singin' Ass," himself.

#####

The heap of items to receive the sun's blessing doubled or tripled over night. Besides the priests' golden necklaces and rings, tribal chieftains deposited their golden crowns and breastplates, as well. Armed guards stood watch over these items, but much of the rest was household goods: bowls, pots, an iron kettle. But in addition, dozens or perhaps hundreds of leather money pouches hung from the skeleton of a holly tree tied to the altar stone, its bare branches bent low under the weight. Cindy could understand the temptation of stealing the priests' and chieftains' gold but stealing from these poor folk who had next to nothing was beyond the pale.

The festivities started before sunrise with a slow, torchlight procession of priests and priestesses, each accompanied by their acolytes. They wore pure white robes embroidered with runic symbols and pictures of magical beasts. One priest wore a dragon on his back. Its flaming breath curled up and over his shoulder. A young priestess with beautiful silver hair woven into intricate, intersecting braids, opened her arms to reveal the outline of a unicorn sewn with golden thread across her chest. The white-on-white image was only discernable when the light of a torch flame danced across the gold thread. Its flickering light gave the magical beast life and movement.

The holy men, women, boys, and girls each added something of their own to the top of the pile of blessings, then formed a half-circle around the altar, facing southeast. Cindy joined the folk who had come from every village and town, some of whom had traveled a week or more, as they formed two rows on either side of a line from the marker stone in the outer ring into the heart of the stone circle.

She heard rustling in the woods and looked on in amazement as Jack Green led his own procession of forest creatures, faeries, wood sprites, and other magical beings from the wood to the edge of the crowd.

No one other than Cindy seemed to notice this strange entourage. In fact, when she poked the woman standing next to her and nodded toward them, the other woman shooed Cindy away with a wave of her hand. When she looked back, Jack met her eye, winked, and his entire band faded from view.

That was...amazing. Freaky, but amazing still. Thank-you, Jack.

Whistler, Bard, and Driver positioned themselves along the avenue of people and led them in chants and songs as the sky brightened and the torches were extinguished. Each chant and song had its own rhythm, *clap, clap, clap, clap-clap-clap-clap*, or *hum, hum, hum-hum-hum, hum, hum*. The rhythms were all in seven-time, but one in particular tickled Cindy's memory. A remembrance overtook her sight and mind. A memory of being surrounded by shelf upon shelf of record albums climbing to the ceiling when all sound was absent except for a raspy voice singing of maids dancing and bells chiming.

She mentally grasped for the image as the memory faded. *I must remember where I was before I was here. It's become so easy to be here in this strange, foreign place that every day feels more and more like home. But it isn't and I've got to remember that.*

Cindy's heart pounded with anticipation when the sun peaked above the gap between the distant mountain peaks. Its first rays shone down the path between the people onto the marker stone, whose long shadow covered the blessings heaped on the altar at the center of the stone ring. The crowd fell silent, and Cindy felt the collective excitement grow. Whistler, Bard, and Driver fell silent, also, as the oldest of the priests in the innermost ring began striking a bell. The other priests and priestesses followed suit, and a riotous clamor of ringing bells enveloped the scene.

As the sun climbed higher, revealing its fat belly, the marker stone's shadow shrank. It withdrew, scurrying back toward its origin while it grew ever darker. Looking into the blackness, Cindy imagined she saw writhing demons and monsters of all sorts held captive by the blazing sun within the shadow's depths.

The tip of the marker shadow finally reached the top of the blessings, and the entire assembly took a sharp intake of breath, which they held until the blackness descended and was replaced by a dazzling brightness reflecting off the priests' gold. The crowd's held breath exploded into cheers. Whistler struck up a jaunty tune, and what a moment before had been a silent, solemn congregation, became a dancing, clapping, and singing party.

Throughout the day, the sun shone down upon the people's most prize possessions and the party continued. From the encampments, people brought meats, cheeses, fruits, and hearty root vegetables, accompanied, of course, by wines, beer, and mead. Chanteur made his rounds with his magical, ever-filling cup, accepting a small copper coin whenever offered. Several times, Cindy saw him paying special attention, and offering free swallows to the guards watching the priests' and chieftains' gold.

Cindy kept a low profile, not wanting anyone from the troupe other than Whistler to see her. She ate a late lunch with the family she met on the road the day before and verified that they had spread the warning of a likely attack she had given them the previous night. They assured her that all were informed and ready.

When Whistler offered her a cup of wine, she eyed it suspiciously, then returned his smile.

"When will they come?" she asked.

"I'm guessing just after the sunset ceremony. People will start retrieving their blessings once the sun is down."

She nodded toward Chanteur, who was handing his cup to one of the guards. "Is that a problem?"

Whistler shook his head and chuckled. "The thing about a magical cup that keeps refilling itself is you never know how much anyone drinks…if they drink at all."

The guard wiped his mouth and clapped Chanteur on the shoulder, who carried his cup to the next one. Gripping his pike tightly, the guard spat out what little of the sleeping draught had passed his lips, then nodded toward Whistler.

#####

Whistler's timing was spot-on. At sunset, a ceremony which was a mirror image of the earlier one began. It differed from the earlier one, not just in the crowd's position at the opposite side of the stone circle, but also in the organization and lack of solemnity of the people. The guards, having vacated their posts, seemed to laze about, some even lying down as if to sleep. The townsfolk, many of whom were well into their cups, paid little heed to the chants of the priests. After all, the sun had blessed their pots, tools, and pouches all day. Instead, they waited impatiently for it to set so they could reclaim their good fortune and get on with the night's festivities.

The bells began ringing again when the sun's squashed form first touched the horizon. The western marker stone's shadow already stretched most of the way to the blessings pile in the center of the rings. As the darkness inched toward the hoard, Cindy again saw those menacing shapes within the blackness. She felt a sense of foreboding emanating from their faces, their eyes wide with excitement and anticipation. By the reaction of the raucous crowd, though, no one else saw the danger.

The assembled folk grew silent, and the demons' countenances changed from feral excitement to rage as a priestess, her diaphanous gown fluttering in the evening breeze, led a line of six other priestesses and seven young girls, all dancing a complex step in seven-time to Whistler's flute. They wove an interlocking pattern around the blessings until the tip of the western marker stone's shadow licked the base of the blessings pile. Then they stopped and joined hands, forming a pattern that Cindy instinctively recognized as an ancient rune of suppression.

How do I know that? It's magic, I guess.

Agonized cries erupted from the shadow-held demons, a collective shriek of anguish and rage, as Whistler's final trilling note faded into the priestesses' chant. The now-rapt crowd quickly took up the chant. Staring into the inky shadow, Cindy saw chains appear and bind each demon.

The tired, red and bloated sun hung in place for a long breath, then plunged down below the horizon. The shadow, which only a moment ago was terrifying and sinister, shot upwards and spread outwards to engulf the hoard. In the resulting gloom, Cindy's eyes dazzled.

At that instant, the attack came.

Ten riders broke from the cover of the forest, followed by at least twice that number of men on foot. Cindy screamed a warning and Whistler let loose a whooping siren note from his flute. The revelers were already in motion, however.

While the women swept up the children and carried them out of the inner rings to the encampments, the men bolted for the blessings pile. To her amazement, Cindy saw them cast aside the golden riches and grab instead their pitchforks, scythes, axes, and shovels. Thus armed, the townsfolk turned as one to face the onrushing attack.

Though outmatched in weapons, nearly a hundred civilian men stood steadfast, and the corps of wide-awake guards joined them. Facing the line of armed men arrayed against them, the horses, and their riders, none of whom had ever been trained in the art of cavalry, turned aside rather than plunging into the briar of simple tools yielded by desperate farmers, smiths, and herdsmen.

Their shock force having broken ranks, the attackers on foot stumbled and paused, waiting for instructions. The bandits' leader, whom Cindy recognized from the clearing in the woods as the captain of the castle guard, yelled commands to his men. He rallied his horsemen, leading them in a flanking maneuver, and exhorted his men on foot to advance.

Pikes and swords against pitchforks? And with the cavalry circling around to attack from behind, these poor folk don't stand a chance.

Coryphee interrupted Cindy's dire thoughts by grabbing her arm.

"Come on, Girlie. We've a job ta do."

Cindy yanked her arm free and turned on the other woman.

"I won't help you steal from these poor folk," she said through clenched teeth.

"I'm not heppin' that bastard Chanteur," she spat. "His schemin' woulda got us all strung up." She reached for Cindy's arm again, but again Cindy snatched it away. "Look," Coryphee said and flicked her head.

Over her shoulder, Cindy saw dozens of women, having removed their children to safety, running full tilt to where the horsemen were making a wide sweeping maneuver.

Coryphee thrust a cord strung with brightly colored ribbons and banners into Cindy's hand. She recognized them as decorations strung on the troupe's wagon. Without another word, Coryphee ran toward the advancing wave of horses. It took Cindy a moment to realize that the crowd of women who were also running to meet the attackers all carried something similar. She saw red, yellow, and blue ribbons, woven blankets, and even white shifts grasped in desperate, yet determined hands. Understanding dawned and, with a mixture of joy and fear in her heart, Cindy took off in Coryphee's wake.

Nothing is fiercer than a lioness or mama bear protecting her cubs. Nothing, perhaps, other than mothers, wives, and daughters defending their loved ones.

Cindy and Coryphee joined the line forming between galloping horses and their menfolk. They held their makeshift banners high and waved them in the gathering darkness. Faced with a wall of riotous shapes and colors swooping and dancing before them, the horses reared, throwing most of their riders to the ground, and galloped away in terror. A cheer went up from the line, and the women fell upon the unhorsed riders like a hive of angry bees.

Expecting a bloodbath, Cindy instead saw the women, not stabbing the attackers with kitchen knives, but quickly trussing them up like holiday turkeys. When she brandished her own knife, one of the other women stayed her hand.

"We give life, Missy, we don' take it."

Another piped up with a laugh, "Unless it be a hen for the pot, eh?"

With eight of the ten horsemen secured, and the ones who fled lost in the darkness, Cindy turned her attention to the men's battle.

The blood on the ground was black as ink. Men had fallen on both sides, but Cindy was shocked to see more armored attackers lying still than defenders.

"These men 'ave fought mor'n one battle for their lords," Coryphee whispered in Cindy's ear. "I wager none o' 'ese fat castle guards 'ave."

"So, you recognize them, too?"

"Aye. 'At bastard singer tol' me o' his deal wit' 'em after we fled the castle." Coryphee hung her head and sighed. "I shoulda stopped 'im then." She choked back a sob. "Now look at what he's wrought."

Cindy couldn't bring herself to feel anything but contempt for the woman. "Speaking of which, where is Chanteur? And why didn't his sleeping draught work on the guards?"

"The thing 'bout a ever-fillin' magic cup is—"

"Yeah, yeah, 'you can't tell how much someone drinks from it.'"

They both scanned the skirmish line, but it had grown almost fully dark. Then, as if by command, the defenders' line parted and a lone figure burst through. The defensive line immediately reformed, leaving the single attacker alone as he ran for the blessings.

Cindy started toward the thief, but Coryphee and another woman held her back. As if orchestrated by some stage director, a person stepped from behind the hoard to block Chanteur's path. The long, thin weapon he brandished marked him.

Cindy gasped, "Whistler." She tried again to run to his aid, but more women came forward to hold her in place.

"This is how it must end," Coryphee said in a voice that wasn't her own. Murmurs of agreement came from all around her. Even the men, having subdued or driven off all the other attackers, turned as one to watch the single combat play out. The older women who had been guarding the children came forward carrying torches. They passed them out as everyone pressed forward, forming another ring around the two combatants.

Seeing who the lone defender was, Chanteur stopped and let out a sneering laugh. He strutted in a circle around Whistler, then, without a word, a dagger flashed in the torchlight. Whistler, brandishing his long flute as a quarterstaff, easily parried the knife thrust, and spun away, but not before delivering a rap to the side of his attacker's head.

The sneer disappeared from Chanteur's face and rage replaced it. With a feint to his right, which Whistler flicked his flute to block, Chanteur flipped his weapon to his left hand. A gasp of horror escaped Cindy as Chanteur plunged the left-handed thrust deep into Whistler's side.

The crowd reacted with a collective gasp, and Cindy screamed, "NO!" She broke free of the arms holding her as Whistler fell backwards. Blood, shiny black in the light of the torches flowed freely from his wound. Chanteur stepped menacingly over him as Whistler's right hand clawed uselessly for his flute, which lay just out of his reach.

With a horrible look of glee, Chanteur gripped his dagger with both hands and raised it above his head, readying it for the *coup de grâce*.

As the knife descended, Cindy smashed into his side, sending them both flying to the dusty ground. The impact sent Chanteur's dagger flying, but it also dislocated Cindy's shoulder. Her left arm hung uselessly at her side and knowing that she had only seconds before the initial numbness yielded to excruciating pain, Cindy grabbed Whistler's flute from the ground and turned to find Chanteur scrambling for his dagger.

With no thought, just a mindless mixture of rage, hate, and an overwhelming need to protect this man who she knew in a flash of insight had orchestrated this entire battle scene, Cindy swung his flute, a hollowed-out branch from the hardest ash tree, down onto the back of Chanteur's head.

The momentum of her mighty stroke spun her off her feet, and she landed directly on her damaged shoulder. Through the resultant blaze of pain, just before blacking out, she saw Chanteur collapse face forward into the dirt and heard a triumphant cheer rise from hundreds of throats.

Chapter 8

Whistler's Tune

ain. Searing into her brain, obliterating all other sensation. A red haze obscuring her sight. The pounding of her pulse in her ears, blocking every other sound. Pain so intense she smelled it, tasted its raw, bitterness on her tongue. Her head swam as the world spun around her. Her dry throat croaked out a pitiful scream, and she tried to push away the tormentors who rolled her onto her back and lifted her useless arm. Someone held her down, and another pinned her kicking legs. Then the world went white for an instant.

When the flair of agony faded, so did the red haze obscuring her vision. Gentle hands swaddled her arm in a sling tied tightly against her body.

"Ya did ya'self a number on 'at shoulder," Coryphee said. "But if nothin's torn, you'll be good as new in no time."

"Whistler?" Cindy's voice croaked, and Coryphee tipped a water skin into her mouth.

She frowned and shook her head. "It's bad. 'is chest is bubblin' and he's spittin' blood."

"Let me see. Where is he?" Cindy's tone was so insistent that those tending to her didn't hesitate. They helped her sit up, then kneel over Whistler, who lay next to her. It was as Coryphee said. His breathing rattled. With every inhale, only the left side of his chest rose while bubbles popped from the wound in his right side. When he exhaled, more bloody bubbles formed on his lips.

Desperate, Cindy looked around and her eyes fell on the broken pieces of Whistler's flute.

"Give me that piece," she said to the woman—Lori, she thought her name was—closest to the shard she wanted. Too confused to argue, Lori passed the three-inch tube to Cindy.

"His blood is collecting inside his chest." She pushed lightly on a soft bulge that had formed under the skin of his side. "We have to give it a way to get out. Then we can re-inflate his lung."

She spun the flute shard in her hand and held the sharply pointed broken end against the pocket of blood.

"Hold him. This is gonna hurt." Coryphee and Lori leaned their weight onto his shoulders and hips. "I need pieces of the cleanest cloth you have," Cindy said to a young girl hovering at the edge of the circle of onlookers who looked like she wanted to help. "Hurry!"

Without a word, the girl lifted her skirt and tore a strip off the hem of her shift. With teeth and strong fingers, other women tore the fabric into small square patches.

Cindy beckoned the girl closer. "Okay. When I jab this in, the blood will pour out, then you need to pack those into the wound. Got it?" The girl drew a sharp breath, then nodded.

Without another word, Cindy jabbed the sharp end of the flute shard into Whistler's side. The fountain of blood that resulted hit Cindy full in the chest and splashed up onto her neck and face. The other women gasped, and at least one shrieked, but the girl was steadfast, and when Cindy nodded to her, she carefully but firmly tucked the squares of cloth into the knife wound.

Within a few seconds, the flow of blood through the tube slowed to a trickle, then to only a few residual drops.

Cindy met the girl's eyes. "Good job," she whispered, bringing a joyful smile to the girl's face. "But we're not done yet. Hold that fast."

Rising to her feet, Cindy wobbled a bit, then stepped around to Whistler's other side.

"Now we have to re-inflate his punctured lung," she said to no one in particular. With her free hand, she arched Whistler's neck, pinched his nose shut, and covered his mouth with her own. Three quick breaths and a long one later, and both sides of his chest rose evenly again.

The onlookers stood in awe and Cindy heard mumblings of "Breath of life" and "healer," but also "witch."

"It's not magic, it's first aid," she growled in response to the last.

Cindy sat back on her heels and watched as Whistler's chest rose and fell. She smiled at the girl, who still held her hand pressed against the wound, then up to Coryphee.

"Bind that up," she said.

Coryphee nodded and tied the wadding in place with a strip torn from her own shift.

"I don't know what to do about infection," Cindy muttered to herself.

Whistler's eyes fluttered, and he whispered, "Don't worry. It's magic."

#####

Whistler drifted in and out of consciousness through the first night, his breathing becoming labored, and blood seeped from his wound. Cindy tended to him while Bard and Coryphee conducted a frantic search of the troupe's kit. They found what they were looking for hidden under the floorboards of the wagon. When they presented the Wondrous Cup to its rightful owner, the High Priestess, now wearing a golden headdress and breastplate, she snatched it from them, and held it to her chest lovingly. Murmuring incantations and swirling her finger in its bowl, she manifested a silver elixir that glowed with an internal light. When the cup was full, she carried it reverently to where Whistler lay.

"It's a healin' 'lixir," Coryphee said when Cindy eyed the cup suspiciously.

"'Tis magic, Sister," the High Priestess whispered. "The strongest I can manage." She looked around the field, where injured men moaned, and their wives and daughters tried to follow Cindy's "healin' teachin's".

The High Priestess continued, "We've much work ta do, startin' with the first among 'ese heroes."

Whistler half-opened his eyes and tried to sit up. Cindy and Coryphee quickly reached in to support him. The High Priestess touched the cup to his lips, then tipped it, pouring a strong draught into his mouth. Whistler sputtered and a few drops dribbled onto his chin, but then he swallowed and sighed. Nodding, he opened his mouth again, and this time gulped down as much as he could. When he finally pushed the cup away, he made a disgusted face.

"Ugh, that tastes terrible."

But then he smiled his thanks to the High Priestess. She nodded and, with the ever-filling cup in hand, made for the next victim.

"See? Told you it's magic," he whispered to Cindy. Their eyes met and locked.

It's now or never, she thought.

She bent and lightly touched her lips to his. When he responded lovingly, firmly pressing his lips to hers, her heart nearly beat out of her chest. She lost herself in their kiss.

When they, at last, parted, Whistler offered a wistful smile, then closed his eyes and fell back asleep.

"Well, it's about damn' time," Coryphee muttered.

#####

The solstice festival lasted through the week. On the seventh day, the first to leave were the herdsman and their families, returning to their cattle. The shepherds left next to relieve those who had remained behind to tend the flocks. Each came and paid their respects to Whistler, who had recovered miraculously quickly from his wounds, bringing wine and mead. To Cindy, who nursed him with newfound feelings that surprised and delighted her, they brought cakes and fruits collected from their meager provisions. Those who had nothing gathered wildflowers from the fields. Each pushed their youngest daughters forward to present their gifts to Cynthia the Fearless.

At this rate, I'll be able to open a florist shop. Or a Whole Foods.

Coryphee, her ever-present surliness having evaporated when the soldiers marched Chanteur and his living accomplices off to face the king's judgement, doted on them both like a mother hen.

When the last stragglers had gone, Cindy helped Coryphee pack up the wagon while Driver hitched up Horse. Bard tuned his mandolin by ear, then played a simple scale. A set of piercing, off-key notes followed.

"Not quite yet," Cindy heard Bard say as she rounded the wagon to see what was making the annoying noise.

Bard and Whistler sat knee-to-knee on the ground. Whistler held the remnants of his flute, which Cindy had broken over Chanteur's hard head, and was whittling thin flakes from it.

"Try it now," he said, and Bard played his scale again.

This time, the tones matched exactly, though an octave apart. Both men smiled, and Bard launched into a fast, dancing tune. Whistler followed along on his newly crafted fife for a few bars, then broke into a trilling solo that had Driver beating a rhythm on the side of the wagon while the women danced.

Coryphee's surprisingly angelic voice took up the melody and Bard added clear and strong harmonies. Cindy grabbed her tambourine and twirled about, feeling as free and at home as she ever had. When the song ended with hugs and laughter, a new troupe was born.

I could…I could live this life with these people. With him.

With her gaze firmly on Whistler, Cindy heard someone clapping behind her. Spinning around, it didn't surprise her to see Jack Green, his staff tucked under one arm, smiling, and offering his applause.

"Shouldn't you be asleep?" she asked.

"Had ta ask if ya've found yer Way, yet."

Cindy looked at the troupe, who were finishing their preparations. No one else seemed to notice Jack's presence. Her gaze lingered on Whistler, again.

"I just may have."

Jack smiled knowingly, then his expression became cautious. "You may not be the only one here seeking their Way," he said enigmatically, then his broad smile returned. "What should you follow?" he asked, a lilt in his voice.

"My heart." Cindy returned his smile, then turned at the sound of Coryphee calling her name. "Be right there," she said.

When she turned back to thank him, Jack was nowhere to be found. With a nod, Cindy returned to her chores. Her heart was light, but still a nagging doubt colored her joy.

Yes, Mr. Whistler. What is the Way that you seek?

Chapter 9

Steps of a Lifetime

here does he go at night?

Whistler's nightly disappearances, which she had barely noticed before, intrigued and concerned Cindy now that they spent their days together, either walking along behind the wagon, or laughing and making music atop it.

Despite the growing closeness between them, they had never even kissed again. Every time she thought they might, a curtain seemed to drop between them—a diaphanous barrier preventing each of them from confessing their true feelings. When she asked him indirectly about his sojourns, he ignored her, deflecting the conversation to some other subject. So, as they trailed the wagon alone, she decided it was time to get some answers.

"Where do you go every night?" she asked as they walked along a dusty valley road.

He responded immediately, as if he had prepared his answer ahead of time. "I just take a walk to clear my head—so I can sleep."

It's not very effective, she thought.

Cindy still slept in the wagon, but both Bard and Driver complained about Whistler's dreaming mumblings.

"Does it help?"

He snorted a laugh. "Not really. Probably makes it worse."

Cindy hesitated, but then plunged forward. "Can I come with you?"

Whistler hesitated. He hadn't prepared for the conversation to take this turn.

"That would be…counter-productive," he said. "No offense," he added to soothe the effect of his words.

Cindy didn't take offense. That she was the cause of his turmoil was somehow reassuring.

"I understand," she whispered. "Every night, I dream about you even before I fall asleep."

Whistler hanging his head and sighing was not the reaction she was hoping for, so she kept her next thoughts to herself.

Why can't I just tell him how I feel? Why won't he tell me how he feels? What is holding him back? It can't be another woman, can it? Certainly not Coryphee. They're friends, but there's been no hint of anything else. I know so little about him, and he won't tell me much when I ask. I know this, though. He doesn't belong in this world any more than I do.

In Cindy's mind, she tried to balance the diminishing hope for a mutual declaration of love against the crushing fear of an outright rejection. The more the likelihood of Whistler falling into her arms shrank, the more precarious that balance became. Cindy trudged along the dusty road in silence.

#####

Bard and Driver's snores made a strange harmony and Coryphee had already retired to the wagon.

"Good night," Cindy said as Whistler banked the campfire's coals against the night air. He mumbled something in return as she climbed the steps to the wagon. Stepping inside, she closed the door, but stood on tiptoe to peak through its high window. As expected, Whistler looked around the campsite, then strode toward the edge of the clearing.

As silently as she had practiced, she slipped out the door and back down the steps, then followed him into the wood.

The moon was half-full, a broken disk hanging high in the sky. Her eyes quickly adjusted to the forest gloom and Cindy made out a faint glow advancing along a game trail ahead of her. Following the yellowish light of Whistler's fife held high above his head was easy. Doing so as quietly as possible, not so much. The snap of a twig beneath her boot brought Whistler to a halt. His head swiveled side to side while Cindy, only a dozen yards behind, held her breath.

After a few seconds, he shrugged and continued. Cindy let him get another ten steps ahead before moving to follow. That's when she noticed something strange happening to her and the surrounding forest. Just like the time before when she followed him through the woods, she felt a disorienting vertigo that pounded inside her head and made her nauseous.

With each step Whistler took, the surrounding trees morphed and twisted. Young saplings grew to towering heights, replacing their ancient brethren, who toppled, rotted, and crumbled to dust. In silence, as if fast-forwarding a movie, the forest aged, its denizens cycling through entire lifetimes as this most enigmatic man strode forward.

Cindy, at first terrified by the scene playing out around her, hurried to keep up, never straying from the twisting path through the woods for fear of losing her own lifetime in Whistler's strides. The imposed silence extended to her own progress as she and her quarry passed through the centuries.

A dozen more strides, and the woods thinned to openness. To her amazement, Cindy saw rows of electric lights in the clearing ahead. With another step, she saw his life unfold before him like a play on a stage.

Whistler as a college student shyly approaching a beautiful chestnut-haired young woman…The two of them laughing over beers, then sharing a bed…Whistler on one knee holding a small box while the woman, hand over her mouth cried and nodded…Dressed in a tuxedo and flanked by his buddies standing at the altar of a small church as the would-be bride's father walked down the aisle alone, shaking his head…Then his best friend consoling him in the same empty church.

Oh my God, she thought. *His fiance left him at the altar and he's trying to find his Way back to her.*

Devastated, and abandoning her attempts at stealth, Cindy advanced to the edge of the forest and gazed at a twenty-first century suburban housing development. Immediately before her, not twenty steps away across its backyard, stood a small split-level house. A wide window revealed a dining room and beyond, a comfortable living room. Whistler stood, motionless, as he waited for her to approach.

"Hi, Tornado Cindy here again," she whispered meekly.

Still staring at the house, he reached for her hand.

"I'm glad you came, my Tornado of the Heart." He dipped his head, but still didn't meet her gaze. "Just give me a minute, please."

When he let her hand go and stepped forward, anger swelled inside her. "Why, so you can try to win her back—again? Like you do every night?"

Whistler stopped and his shoulders sagged. "I stopped trying to win her back months ago," he said. "Since I met you, I've been trying to say 'Goodbye.'"

Without another word, he crept forward, hunched low avoiding the trapezoids of light that shone through the windows. He pulled his feathered cap from his head, twisting it in his hands as he peeked into the dining-room window.

From her vantage point, Cindy could see a table set for two. A woman, the one from the vision, her long hair falling about her shoulders, entered from the adjacent kitchen and, striking a match, lit the candles in their brass holders.

Whistler's shoulders rose as he took a deep breath and stood, stepping into the light. But at that moment, the woman turned at some sound from the front of the house. A tall man came through the front door, and she rushed to greet him. His clean-cut black hair framed a handsome face, and the cut of his business casual clothes revealed a fit, well-muscled body.

They embraced. They kissed, their lips lingering lovingly. As if pricked by a balloon, Whistler's shoulders collapsed. When the couple parted, he shook his head and shrugged in sorrow, then stepped out of the light back into the shadowed darkness. Cindy saw the woman stop and silently gasp as he disappeared from beyond her window.

Without stopping, Whistler strode right past where Cindy stood, no longer trying to stay hidden.

"Try to keep up," he said without even looking in her direction.

She stood, transfixed, looking at the modern world—her world—beyond the trees. He was ten steps beyond her, and she hadn't moved yet when he stopped and turned to where she stood. Looking to her left, she saw this strange man who seemed to command both time and space, and for whom she felt as she never had for anyone else. Turning to her right, though, she saw the world someone had plucked her from and she knew with a few steps she would be right back, sitting in Pops' favorite overstuffed chair in his music library.

"Or stay here," Whistler said, his voice full of all the sadness in the world. She turned back to see him shrug again, the tears in his eyes shimmering in the moonlight. "It's your choice. Choose your Way."

He extended his hand, the invitation clear.

She glanced again at the modern world, her world, then offered her own shrug and stepped forward to take his hand. Instead of following him back through the woods and the ripples of time he commanded, though, she pulled him into her arms and their lips met. When they breathlessly parted, she smiled slyly and tugged him toward the present.

At first, he resisted her pull, but she squeezed his hand tightly and pulled him into her embrace again, and their lips met, again. This one lingered and, as one, they made a silent decision together. They looked deeply into each other's eyes, and *their* Way became clear. Like a pair of teenagers, they ran hand-in-hand into their future.

Chapter 10

Midnight Embers

heir home is a cabin in a clearing high on a wooded mountain. A country kitchen, two bedrooms, and a loft surround and overlook a cozy room whose focus is a massive stone fireplace. Antique instruments—a drum, a mandolin, and a homemade tambourine adorn the walls. Holding pride of place above the rough-cut wooden mantel are the pieces of a broken wooden flute.

A large cat, with tufted ears and green eyes, yawns, stretches, then resumes its spot, curled in a furry ball, on the wide hearth. A black lab snores lightly next to the overstuffed easy chair where Ian stretches out, flute at hand, watching the dying fire. Flames flare up and die as breezes tickle the last of its embers, signaling the ending of another working day wrapped in warmth and comfort, and love.

For all its rustic charm, however, the cabin has all the amenities a modern life demands. Buried fiber optics tie it into the wide world and Ian's state-of-the-art music studio is steps away in its own soundproof bungalow. The largest room, set off from the others, holds row upon row of sturdy shelves filled to overflowing with records of all sizes, and eras, including the latest album by Ian's band, Whistler's Troupe.

Having finished the last video call of the day, talking about her book of fairytales to yet another internet influencer, Cindy gets ready for bed. The clink of her hairbrush on the antique mahogany desk she uses for a vanity drifts in from the bedroom.

Ian sits quietly, a steaming mug warming one hand while the other scratches the lab between the ears. He hums the melody of a love song, something he seldom writes, anticipation quickening his pulse.

Cindy's voice, subtly inviting, calls him to bed, and he rises, sets the golden toddy on the mantel, and answers her summons.

THE END

AUTHOR'S NOTE

Well, that was fun…for me at least. I hope it was fun for you, as well. As I mentioned in the Preface, this narrative was my attempt to stitch together the themes, characters, mood, and stories contained in Jethro Tull's album "Songs from the Wood." Ian Anderson's music and lyrics have always transported me, although not quite as drastically as Cindy was, to a fantasy land of fairies, Green Men, magic, and most of all, music.

Of course, "Songs from the Wood" is available wherever you buy or stream music—does anyone buy music anymore? As the dad of a working musician, that's a troubling question. Also, if you want to explore Tull's or Ian Anderson's music further, just go to https://JethroTull.com.

As always, you can find me, my flash fiction blog, newsletter sign-up, and anything else I post at https://robjohnsonwriting.net

Tales from the Wood

Thanks, again, Faithful Reader, for taking some
time out of your day to spend with me and this
ancient form of mental telepathy called storytelling.

Faithfully,

R.A. (Rob) Johnson
Pennsylvania, U.S.A.
July 2022

ACKNOWLEDGEMENTS

First, I'd like to thank Ian Anderson and the many members of Jethro Tull, past and present, for a lifetime of musical memories, not the least of which stem from "Songs from the Wood."

Thanks, as always, go to my beta readers, Carly Johnson, Sarah Inforzato, and Glenn Bresciani. Your feedback and suggestions have made this infinitely better.

Thanks, also, to Elizabeth Nightingale Devine (I so love your name!) for endless encouragement over the years, and especially your enthusiasm when I first told you about my crazy idea to write a novella based on an obscure forty-five year old progressive rock album. Keep Seeking!

I can't say enough how happy I am with the wonderful cover art and interior chapter illustrations done by Illustrators of the Future winner, Anthony Moravian. They bring my pedestrian text to life. Anthony is at https://moravianart.com, or on https://Reedsy.com.

As does the narrator of the audio version of "Tales," Naomi Mayo. Even after the dozens of times I've read, re-read, edited, or listened to the book, your performance transports me. You can find Naomi (and hire her!) at https://www.naomimayo.com, or where I found her, on https://FindawayVoices.com.

And a shout out to Vandy Pacetti-Donelson, whose beautifully illuminated letters introduce each chapter.

Finally, thanks to the folks at ProWritingAid.com, whose tools make my barely intelligible musings actually readable.

To connect with me, check out my website www.RobJohnsonWriting.net. There you will find my blog, which contains dozens of flash fiction pieces, and you can join his email list to get monthly newsletters, bonus stories, and special offers.

I am also active in the Fiction Writers Group on Facebook, the APEX Writers Group, Superstars Writing Seminars (yay, Tribe!), the Western Colorado University's Creative Writing/Publishing MA program, the Pottstown Writers Group, The Writers of the Future Contests, and various other challenges and competitions.

You can contact me directly at rob@robjohnsonwriting.net.

An audio version of this book, narrated by Naomi Mayo, is available.

Midnight Embers

Other Titles by R.A. Johnson

FICTION

The Enclave Series

#1 *The Templar Lance*

#2 *Lady 355: Mother of Freedom*

Ghost Stories

The Ghost of Mackey House

NON-FICTION

Mental Crudites – Appetizers for the Creative Mind
Series

#1 *Helping Science Fiction Writers Get Their Stories Off
the Ground*

www.ingramcontent.com/pod-product-compliance
Lightning Source LLC
Chambersburg PA
CBHW022056050726
47591CB00002B/572